"Have a seat." She gave the bed a pat with her open hand. "Take a load off." She took a damp towel out of her beach bag and hung it over the wicker love seat by the window. "I love this old wicker." The sides of her mouth worked up in a sad little smile and she bent over to rummage through her bag on the seat of the little couch. "Oh sit down, please."

"We really can't. We have to go," Naomi said. "Ginny, let's go." I saw her slip the notebook in the pocket of her bermuda shorts before we headed for the door.

"Oh have a seat anyway." The woman patted the bed again. "Sit, sit," she said as if it were an invitation to a tea party, but she'd taken up a small black revolver from her bag. As far as I was concerned, it put her sincerity into question, but I told her I thought we'd stay since she'd asked so nicely. I dropped myself on the bed; the box springs thumped and creaked and Naomi's face looked like warm death under her tan.

THE LAVENDER HOUSE MURDER

A VIRGINIA KELLY MYSTERY

NIKKI BAKER

BOOKS BY NIKKI BAKER

In the Game
The Lavender House Murder
Long Goodbyes

THE
LAVENDER HOUSE
MURDER

A VIRGINIA KELLY MYSTERY

NIKKI BAKER

The Naiad Press, Inc.
1993

Printed in the United States of America on acid-free paper
First Edition
First Printing June, 1992
Second Printing December, 1993

Edited by Katherine V. Forrest
Cover design by Pat Tong and Bonnie Liss
    (Phoenix Graphics)
Typeset by Sandi Stancil

Library of Congress Cataloging-in-Publication Data

Baker, Nikki, 1962–
    The lavender house murder / by Nikki Baker.
        p.   cm.
    ISBN 1-56280-012-4
    I. Title.
PS3552.A4327L3   1992
813'.54—dc20   91-33356
                                                          CIP

Acknowledgements

For Margaret, Judith, and for Paula Walowitz, a great astrologer.

With thanks again to Val, and Cynthia, and to Lori, Sue and Renee.

Disclaimer

This book is a work of fiction. Any similarity in name, description, or history of characters in this book to actual individuals either living or dead is purely coincidental.

I am no goddess/so you've said, but worship

—Victoria Brownworth
Novena

I

July 18

You bitch. I know where you're staying now. You can't hide and I'm going to make you sorry for what you've done. I have waited a long time to have my retribution.

II

I had spent the better part of the morning sitting at a beat-up wooden table in the conference room of the Provincetown Police Station, wishing I were someplace else while various policemen came and went. Anyplace else would have been fine: back with my ex-girlfriend, Emily, watching the Cubs lose again while the wind off the lake made dust devils out of the trash in the gutters. Back with my ex-lover Susan (the bone of contention over whom Emily had walked out on me almost a year ago), rolling around under the recessed lighting set in Susan's fourteen-foot vaulted ceilings. The craziness of my relationships wasn't looking so bad when compared objectively with the alternatives.

What I knew for sure was this: if I hadn't let Naomi talk me into a Provincetown vacation, someone else would be sitting here with the cops. Someone else would be feeling vaguely unsettled in her own existence and I would be reading about it in the Chicago gay rags as if it were an earthquake in India or a little flood in the Philippines. I could turn the page and go on to the next heart-wrenching, sick-making headline. And if it all got too awful to think about I could turn the page again and read the phone-sex advertisements or the personal ads for more commonplace horrors.

But Naomi Wolf had a knack for calling trouble, then stepping aside; and the situation fairly stank of her dubious kind of kismet or rather, my own in knowing her. When the meteor struck, it was my kind of luck to be standing in the way. So, on the occasion of my first visit to the Provincetown police station, I was there to report a corpse.

I had first noticed it while I was running down Commercial Street. The leg was a flaw in the sweep of my vision, a blemish at its corner, the way you might catch the belly of a fish floating white side up

in a lake where you are planning to swim, the way
you let your eye take you down the chalky stomach
to the quiet gills and the sightless, staring eye. Your
own eyes can betray your sense of well-being by
calling you quickly and against your will to the
faults in a smooth clean surface when a minute ago
everything seemed just fine. This was the way I had
come upon the remains of Joan. Looking harder as I
came up close and squinting my eyes as if I were
waiting for a spot on the floor to move. Then
bending towards the gravel, bracing my hands on my
thighs the way I'd bent to catch my breath when
Joan and I had jogged together the day before, I
was retching sick. I had thought of Joan often since
we'd met — but not like this and I stood away from
her so that I didn't step in the blood.

Joan had been shot chest-high at the distance of
a friendly handshake, then again in the head while
the gun sat flush against the side of her face. Like
the special effects from a B-grade movie, black
gunpowder tattoos were splattered in deco-like
accidental paint against the pallor of her skin. Her
stare had the frozen surprise of car headlights left
on long and her tank top rode halfway up her chest,
above a stomach as flat and white as winter. Her
blood had settled in the backs of her arms and legs.
Leached out of her veins when she died, it stained
her skin like one last sunburn. On her left hand
was a bona fide tan line where she'd worn her
diamond ring.

Her hair was clotted with blood gone brown in
the sun. There was a pool of it around her head and
she was black with flies. They had danced on her
face in the shade of half-built Cape Cod vacation

homes, the last frail gasp of Boston's Xerox miracle. Her lips were parted slightly against the gravel. And even in death Joan had managed to look as if she were planning a kiss.

Sheriff Edward Harmon scratched his leg discreetly and we looked at each other across the table. It seemed that while Joan Di Maio had enjoyed the company of many women, on the occasion of her murder the police could find no one in particular to call.

The sheriff ran his hands through his hair from his forehead to the nape of his neck. The hair was thinning and grey, slicked down with something I hadn't thought they sold anymore. He asked me again what I had been doing when I found Joan as if the question was new.

Since 8:30 that morning, Wednesday, the police had been asking me the same questions over and over again. Even they seemed to be getting tired of the answers, so they took turns. The old ones would leave and new ones would take their shift. But the questions didn't change much. What had I been doing when I found Joan? What had I been doing before I found Joan? Why was I doing it? How did I know her?

The first question they asked, of course, was where, but that had been eclipsed by the others after I took them to the construction site. We rode in a squad car, I in the back, two policemen in the front and at least one other car behind us. I didn't mind that this was the biggest news in the last decade for these small town cops, but I didn't like it that I felt more like a convict behind the wire cage than a helpful, upstanding citizen. Next they wanted

4

to know my name and where I was staying and where I lived and what I did for a living there. If they wanted to know whether I'd been breast fed as a baby, they stopped just short of asking. And behind every inquiry was the sneaking suspicion that I had done something wrong. I won't say the cops weren't pleasant enough, but it didn't feel like they were ready to give me any awards for cooperation.

They had asked their questions in various tones of insinuation, as suspicious as stray dogs, from the time I'd come into the station to announce that I'd found a body. And I was starting to get the idea that I was in a lot of trouble or could be without much additional effort.

Harmon asked me again what I was doing in Provincetown and I could honestly answer that I was having one hell of a vacation. But he didn't smile when he told me to start again from the beginning.

III

Provincetown is at the tip of Cape Cod. You can get there on a ferry that runs once a day from Commonwealth Pier in Boston leaving at 9:30 in the morning and returning at 3:30 sharp in the afternoon. It holds a thousand people on three levels with a place for bicycles, luggage, packages, and two white-haired old gentlemen who play dixieland music and take requests. On the way out of Boston Harbor, the captain will give you a history lesson over the public address system. You can stand at the bow of the boat in the wind and your hair will be damp from the spray when you land three hours later; and your head will be filled with local trivia.

There is also a bus that leaves from the Peter Pan Terminal on Atlantic Avenue across from South Station in Boston and stops in front of the Provincetown Chamber of Commerce off Commercial Street. This has the quality of a dusty movie stagecoach because it stops at every hole and crack in the ground from Jam's store in Truro to Denmark's Pharmacy in Dennisport. Additionally, you can flag it down along its route in Chatham and Harwich and Yarmouth where there are no official stops.

If you catch an early bus on a Saturday say, you can get to Provincetown at the same time as the Ferry, in time to have some lunch. If you wait too late, the highway backs up like a two-lane parking lot and God only knows when you'll arrive. Saturdays are especially terrible since all the cottages and condominiums on the Cape rent by the week, Saturday to Saturday.

Given these choices of quaint and charming transportation, of course Naomi had insisted on driving. Nonetheless, our vacation in Provincetown started slowly, largely uneventfully, the way a roller coaster pulls away from the platform, clanking and rattling like an old cattle car until you see the hair-raising drop over the crest of the rickety metal hill.

Five days earlier, owing to the Saturday traffic, Naomi Wolf and I had found ourselves stopped dead at the side of Route 6, halfway to P-town waiting for the water in the radiator of the rental car to quit boiling. Naomi's idea of a drive up the Cape was looking less and less inspired. She was sitting on the car bumper swearing at the highway berm and I was listening.

It took all the emotional energy I could pull together. In the space of the last year, my lover Emily had left and come back and left again. My fling with the very crazy Susan Coogan had been so disillusioning to Em that she could not seem to make up her mind whether to stay with me or go. The boomerang quality of our relationship was wearing me out. Though I couldn't really blame Em. We are what we are and she had a stubborn, Catholic idea of sin, courtesy of her white ethnic upbringing. She was convinced that even if I weren't still sleeping with Susan, I was probably still thinking about it, resurrecting my old indiscretions through memory and lust. Em couldn't help that my fantasy life was as real to her as fire and ice, and we had agreed on separate vacations, conceding that even the most perfect union requires rest.

"What you need is new blood," Naomi had advised me in February. Naomi was my very worst self and I could not help but like her for it. "You need to meet some reasonable women."

I thought Naomi was probably right, but she would have had a lot more credibility if she hadn't been the one who had hooked me up with Susan Coogan and gotten me into this fix to begin with. But I didn't have the heart to fight with her in that respect or any other. Naomi's mind was set on a week in Provincetown. There was nothing to do but ride along in the flow of her enthusiasm, hoping that Provincetown, like most things remembered from Naomi's past, had not taken on a lore that was entirely removed from the physical world. I was hoping mostly that it would not approximate the dirty seaside communities I had toured as a child.

When I was growing up my family had a place, a condominium on the Delaware shore. My mother packed up the car and we went there every summer for ten days. The rest of the time, my father rented it out to people that he knew.

The condo, a short walk from the water, had been sold for years now. It had made my parents' retirement, and the selling price increased their fondness for the place in retrospect. My father even cried after the closing, in the way men do sometimes, with no sound, and tears that filled his eyes up; he blew his nose into his handkerchief and they were gone. His memories were of a middle-class dream achieved, a summer house that represented all the ways an educated black man could participate in America. It didn't matter to him that his was the only black family on ten miles of beach.

My own memories were lukewarm and lonely, as I was an African-American princess with the fatal flaw of kinky hair. What I saw at twelve as the major disadvantage of my race could not be rectified by money or privilege and little black girls with their hair on end do not want to hear about black pride when they are taught on movie screens that what is beautiful is straight and white and western. And the straightening perm I wore, once wet, could never seem to be put right again without the support of heat and rollers, both of which were in short supply at the Delaware beach; and I regretted that first day in the water for the rest of my vacation. In a way that I thought mattered, the trial of my hair made me different from the hundreds of white faces on that dirty stretch of sand.

Growing up, I was alone in regretting my hair as my mother did not like the water. She kept to the sand and her paperback novels. And my younger sister, Adeline, had the kind of hair that black people will sometimes call "good" because it is fine and nearly straight. Wet, it lay smooth against her head; it dried in waves and rings. Strangers stopped to admire Adeline's looks.

My father didn't bother about his own hair except to keep it cut. Though he wanted for his girls hair that was long and loose, as homogenized a look as possible. Hair to hang on our backs and fan out when we turned, like the hair on white women in magazines.

I let him down. My hair was thick and coarse like his, curled up in patterns of its own choosing rather than the ones I tried to make it follow on brush rollers under the heat of a bonnet hair dryer, and so black that it could look almost blue. People said that I favored my father when I was a girl and the remark engendered my dislike. I imagined that with my kinky hair and broad features, I was being told that I looked like a man.

* * * * *

Naomi pushed the stray hair from her brown bob hairdo out of her eyes and kicked the rental tires. Then she settled down on the bumper again to smoke as if the activity had worn her out. Her body was all lines and angles. Chain-smoking kept Naomi thin and caffeine helped level out her temper, but she hadn't had her coffee this morning. She said, "I thought we were going to get to the beach today. It's almost fucking three o'clock."

"Nice mouth, Naomi," I said. "I told you to run the air conditioner. That keeps the car from overheating. It has to do with the compressor." I had heard a woman who looked like she was born under a car hood say this once and it made me feel smart to repeat it. I said, "Maybe it isn't the compressor. How's the oil?" and felt even smarter.

Naomi blew a line of smoke out over her head and got back into the car. She rolled the window down, hung her cigarette out of it and wouldn't be troubled to answer me.

After a while some white girls in a Chevy Blazer with New Jersey license plates saw the hood was up and stopped to help us out. One of them said she knew about cars. The car girl looked under the hood like she was going to work alchemy and Naomi invited herself into the back seat of the Blazer to make time with any one of the women there. If she couldn't get lucky, sure thing Naomi would conclude that they were, none of them, her type. Naomi was a practical girl; she didn't want what she couldn't have. It was something about her I could admire, but otherwise Naomi was pretty short on virtues.

"Can you fix it?" I said.

The car girl wore a red Hawaiian shirt and rugby shorts which rode up on her legs. She rolled her shoulders. "There's not much to fix, babe. You just wait till it cools off." She touched the radiator top with her fingertips and then smiled. Her nails were bitten to the nubs and the dirt underneath made her look authentic as a grease monkey. "How long have you been here?"

"I don't know." I guessed: "An hour." Naomi was still smoking in the Blazer. "Half a pack of cigarettes?"

"Well your radiator's cooled off now."

The car girl swaggered back to her car. She took a plastic jug from the back of the Blazer and poured some water into a tank under our hood. The other girls, one with curly red hair and a heavy one in a spandex tube top, got out of the Blazer nodding their approval. Naomi was in hot pursuit of the curly-haired one. She followed them back over to the car and we all stood around like armchair generals, watching the car girl pour the water into what I took for the radiator tank.

"That should do it." The car girl brushed her hands off on her shorts, and the other girls bobbed their heads some more as if they'd done something.

"Thanks a lot," said Naomi. She was talking to the girl with the curly hair. Naomi asked if they were headed for P-town.

The heavy girl answered. Yes, they were. "We're

renting a house near Herring Cove beach. We're staying a week, till next Saturday," the heavy girl said.

"Maybe we'll see you again sometime. Or maybe not." Naomi yawned like she'd given the curly-headed girl her best efforts such as they were and they had better be enough. They weren't.

The heavy girl said, "We'll be at the beach. Look for our volleyball net, if you want to find us."

The car girl winked at me and Naomi rolled her eyes.

The New Jersey women started back to their Blazer with the curly-hair's hips swinging to and fro around her waist while she walked.

"Thanks again." Naomi watched the curly-headed girl's behind. "Thanks so very much," she said.

The car girl opened the door. She sat down in the front passenger's seat and winked again. The car girl had a slow tilted grin that built itself across her face as if she didn't know how it was going to end up. She had eyes as brown and warm as roasted chestnuts. I was betting she had other charms.

She said, "See you around, babe," and then she waved. The curly-headed girl honked twice and pulled the car back into traffic.

"Come on." Naomi got in behind the wheel of our rental. "We don't have all fucking day," she said.

IV

July 19

*I wonder sometimes what your life is like, if you
are happy now that you have made mine unbearable.
I wonder if you ever think of me.*

V

Two hours later, we were still in the same line
of cars pressed bumper to bumper, and only twenty
miles further down the road. Naomi was working out
her aggressions on the car horn and I was watching
the house numbers, having lost sight of the Blazer
some time ago.

Lavender House, where we were booked, sat
across from the community center between The
Bradford Inn and The Shamrock Motel. It was a
sprawling wood mansion, all painted purple in
varying shades with a wide front porch and a
widow's watch on its roof tall enough to have a view

of the bay. A rich man's house some hundred and fifty years ago hemmed in by the low Cape Cod shacks that surrounded it, it had been brought down now to renting by the room.

The old house sat back a good way from the street and its hulk threw shade onto the cracked ribbon of sidewalk that ran along in front. Its white picket fence disappeared around the side of the house along a gravel driveway and met the road at a hand-lettered sign that read FREE GUEST PARKING.

Naomi conveniently forgot the bags when she went to ring the front door bell. I could hear her swearing as I closed the trunk. And by the time I'd gotten our stuff across the yard, she was squared off on the porch with a tough-looking, middle-aged white woman in batik shorts. The woman wasn't very big, but I thought she could probably take Naomi. If it came to that, I would have liked to have seen it.

The woman on the porch looked mad enough to fight — the veins in her neck stuck out at her shirt collar. She was blocking the entrance to the Lavender House with both arms like George Wallace in front of the schoolhouse door. But she shook my hand by the way of a truce after I'd explained we had a reservation.

"I'm Samantha Flynn," she said, "but most people call me Sam."

She was a handsome woman. Her face was brown from gardening and her hair was poker straight, the color of stainless steel.

Sam pushed some hair behind her ears and put on an expression that was all business. "You can follow me up to your room," she said. When she bent to pick up my bags, she jerked her head in Naomi's direction. "It's been a long time, Naomi." Sam left Naomi's bags on the stoop, but her voice was almost pleasant, though she didn't quite manage a smile.

The room was through the entryway, upstairs and to the end of a long hall, past three other rooms and a back stairway that led, presumably, outside. Sam took the steps two at a time. That made me think she was younger than her hair. She dropped my bags at the door. Then she opened the room with a set of keys from her pocket and pressed them in my hand.

"This is your only set," Sam said, "so don't lose it. I keep an extra for cleaning and I might have another spare, but I'd appreciate it if you didn't make me look for it. The new one is to the deadbolts on the front. The old-fashioned one is to your room."

Sam sneaked a peek at Naomi. It was somewhere between hate and curiosity and I would have been glad to pay a penny for her thoughts. Sam looked back at the floor and scuffed the toes of her canvas sneakers on the wool runner in the hall. Her bony ankles stuck out at the tops of her shoes. "Breakfast is at nine sharp every morning. If you're going to sleep in just let me know, so I won't make extra."

I stowed the keys in my pocket. "All right," I said.

The lock on the door looked to be the original article. Sam watched me as I ran my fingers along the cut glass edges of the doorknob and stuck my head into the room to get the lay of the land. I thought Em would have liked it, the way she read

Metropolitan Home full of tastes she couldn't yet afford. I liked the permanence of the wood headboard on the bed; I liked its weight. The room was filled with things that were built to last in the face of my own rather temporal existence, and the throw-away ethic I'd come to accept as more convenient than old-fashioned commitment.

Both Sam and her house were, in a word, Victorian. Sturdy. They were, it seemed, immovable, a collection of frosted glass shades and dark wood covered over with lace doilies and attitude.

Naomi was already making herself at home, throwing her shirts into the best drawers and claiming all the hangers for her own. It was typical Naomi behavior and I was trying to convince myself that I really *preferred* to live out of my suitcase on vacation. It was almost working. Besides, I didn't hold much hope of getting too comfortable as the bed didn't look big enough for more than two very close friends.

In the drawer of the little dressing table, along with some old lint, was a pen and note-sized pad of purple paper embossed with the Lavender House insignia *LH* like a kind of lesbian Holiday Inn. The only thing missing was the Gideon Bible. But the beaten-down wicker couch by the window had promise, and a door near the bed led to a private bathroom as advertised.

"I'd appreciate it if there was no smoking in the room," Sam said.

I understood it to be a threat, but Naomi seemed blissfully undisturbed. She set her hard-pack of Marlboro Lights down on the top of the dressing table next to her lighter like she was throwing down the gauntlet.

Sam said, "We can settle up downstairs whenever you're ready." She was talking to me. "I've got some tourist information you can have if you want it."

As we went into the front hall, I could hear Naomi swearing. She shut the door hard behind us, I was guessing with her foot. "Yeah, I love you too, you bitch," Naomi said.

Downstairs on the dining room table Sam spread out a map of Provincetown. It was printed on purple paper that matched note pads she'd put in the rooms.

"This is Lavender House." Sam bent over the map and circled the spot with a ballpoint pen. Places of interest were marked, restaurants and bars, women's places. She circled an area northeast down Bradford Street and pointed at it. "That's Herring Cove Beach. Most of the women go there. There's Race Point Beach and some others out of town, but Herring Cove is the lesbian one."

"I've marked the places to eat owned by women and if you want a reservation anywhere, you just tell me at breakfast and I'll call it in for you." Sam produced a copy of *Provincetown Magazine* from the stack of papers on the table and thumbed the pages, talking while she looked for the one she wanted. "There are some shows, too." Sam smiled and pointed to an advertisement. "You've got to see

Hillela, Hillela Hill. She's a comic. I could make a reservation for you tomorrow." Sam turned the page of her magazine to a man who thought he was Judy Garland. "Do you like drag?" she asked me. "Naomi used to like drag shows."

"Where do you know Naomi from?" I said.

"It's a long story." Her voice sounded tired just from thinking about it. "You'd better ask Naomi to tell you that, but I'm surprised she hasn't been over her history yet. You haven't been together long then, have you?"

"No." I laughed. "Not long at all."

"You don't have to tell me your business if you don't want to," Sam said. "But the people who come here, I always get to know them a little. You'll see that at breakfast." She handed over the stack of brochures as if her feelings had been hurt. "Of course, I knew Naomi years ago." She pressed the map of Provincetown onto the top of the pile of tourist information. "So she interests me, you understand?"

Whatever had gone on with her and Naomi, it was still going on from the look of it and I didn't think I wanted to be in the middle. "Naomi and I are just pals." I held up three fingers close together. "Scout's honor." It was all I could remember from eight years of girl scouting besides the girls. "You just must not have known Naomi very well, not to know what she likes."

"People change." Sam's eyes were sad. "You never can tell," she said.

I guessed not.

VI

"Tell me again why you think this girl is your friend Joan Di Maio," Harmon was saying. He was sitting next to me now. I watched him from the side. There was silver stubble on his neck underneath his hair. His hands were big and red and the fuzz on his knuckles looked like frost.

I said, "She's not my friend, exactly." I was talking to Harmon about things we'd talked about before, as slowly as if I were explaining rocket science to a three-year-old. "I know it was her because she has a tattoo on the inside of her thigh."

Harmon wore an expression just short of a leer. I imagined it was a sign of restraint as he probably leered enough to be good at it.

"I'd seen her tattoo before at the beach and I recognized it," I told him, "but she wasn't exactly what you'd call a friend."

It was true. Joan was something between a yen and a mild obsession, somewhere between an itch and a yeast infection. She could make you feel like there was no one else in the world but you and her, and then make you sorry for it. But, that was something about me and about her that I didn't think I ought to share with Sheriff Harmon and I told him again for simplicity's sake that Joan was more of an acquaintance than a friend.

Harmon rolled his head around on his shoulders

and growled at me. "If she wasn't your friend, maybe you'd know if she had any enemies?"

I shook my head. What he asked was hard to answer. Joan liked to feel her power over people — in words, in print, in another woman's body. She had the allure of things that can make you bleed and the kind of looks that are sometimes fatal. Joan could make you both sick and high like a bad drunk, and as it turned out there were probably a lot of reasons someone might want to kill her. But I could only think of two at the time: love or hate. Mixed feelings. I thought it was for Joan that they had coined the expression. At least it pretty much summed up the effect she had had on me.

VII

After we checked in on Saturday, the vacation started turning into the kind I'd hoped for: good weather, slow pace, cold beer. I was ready to forget why I'd had to come without Em. I was ready to forget I was probably about to become single; and that's what it came down to even if I tried to call it "space" and separate vacations. It depressed me so much just to think about having to date again that I was even happy for Naomi to give me a guided tour of Provincetown, or at least the places she remembered from her own personal nostalgic trip; it was better than nothing. The drone of her voice took my mind off my own more recent history and what I judged to be my even more depressing future on the single-lesbian dating circuit.

The thing about dating is that lesbians don't know how to do it. We are a segment of the population that meets and marries, usually briefly, frequently unhappily. Studying us one would think we had a shorter life expectancy than normal human beings. I could count on one hand the years that Em and I had been together, but we owned jointly a leather couch that had cost us as much as an economy car, a dining room set and wedding china. And the longevity of our relationship was nearly a diamond anniversary in lesbian years.

"There are three main streets in P-town," Naomi said, "but traffic only moves down Bradford and Route Six." She pointed to the narrow street beside us where the cars were moving along at a crawl. "Commercial Street, where we are now, runs right along the water on the inner crook of the Cape. Route Six-A splits off on the east end of town where the main trunk goes north; it becomes Bradford Street where we came in. The rest of it turns into Commercial."

She had hold of my arm and was pulling me along with her through the crowd the way that mommies hang onto their toddlers at Marshall Field's Department Store in the Christmas shopping rush. This was her chance to wield the undisputed authority of the people who conduct bus tours. As a lawyer, Naomi couldn't bear to see the opportunity pass. She fairly bubbled over with the joy of being

21

listened to. "Commercial Street is the main shopping district. But it's way too narrow for both people and cars so I cut down the side streets whenever I really want to get anywhere."

Naomi was talking like she had been here just the week before instead of fifteen years ago. In Naomi's mind the world was static until she wanted it to change. It was a trick of perception I would have liked to learn.

"Look, see —" she waved her arm at the little snatches of beach between the storefronts, "— that's Provincetown Bay. When we get about halfway down we'll see MacMillian Wharf. There's this hot dog stand." Naomi paused with her finger on her lower lip as if she were deciding whether or not to let me in on a tremendous opportunity. "When I was in school we used to come up here all the time on the Ferry and sit on the benches further down in front of Town Hall. We'd get a hot dog and watch the girls go by."

Naomi waved her arm again towards the west end of town where Commercial makes a hard jog south towards the water and winds itself past quiet oceanfront residences to the Pilgrim Commemorative Plaque by the breakwater off the highway. Then it meets Route Six-A again and travels north in a loop back up to Highway Six and east up the Cape, back to Boston. Across the breakwater to the west and north are the public beaches of Cape Cod National Seashore: Herring Cove on the western edge and Race Point near the Coast Guard Station and the Provincetown air strip. The break between the beaches is the lighthouse at Race Point which sits at the outer bend of the Cape. To the east is the lighthouse at Wood End and at the furthest southeast tip there is Long Point, site of the Civil War fort and the Pilgrims' first landing.

Now, tourism takes it every year from three thousand residents off-season to sixty thousand people in the eight weeks of the summer, trying the limits of the waste disposal system and the patience of the locals.

People tramped along now by the hundreds beside and around us, blocking traffic, pushing us past the storefronts down the middle of a road that had started as a cattle path. A stationary conversation with a friend could make a bottleneck of cars and people that went on for two blocks. Two gay men in leather walked hand in hand in front of us and the air was warm and wet as a steam bath. Middle-class families were pushing 2.3 children in double strollers and the sounds of buying and selling were everywhere. Three hundred years after the landing of the Mayflower, restaurant windows proclaiming AIR CONDITIONING did a brisk business in season, when Provincetown woke up like Brigadoon.

Naomi and I sat on the end of MacMillian Wharf by the moorings for the fishing boats. I opened the paper around one of her well-remembered coney dogs. She was waving her carry-out bag at the bees. They were slow and high on soda pop from the trash cans along the pier, and I tipped up the end of my beer in its brown paper sack, happy to have something cool in my hand.

"How do you know Sam?" I asked her.

"From a long time ago." Naomi lit another cigarette.

"From school, then?" I asked.

She smoothed her brown hair. "Sam's older than I am, though." The thought seemed to please her. She drew on the last of her cigarette, then threw it like a dart at our reflection in the water. "Are you planning to finish that coney?" She popped my leftovers into her mouth and belched.

I said, "Did you get any on you?"

"Fuck you," said Naomi and I figured I deserved the sentiment.

It was too hot to drink, but I was doing a pretty good job at it — that and watching the people. Provincetown and the Wharf had caught hold of my imagination like the Hoxie Brother's traveling circus that came through my home town every year when I was a kid, set up in a rain-soaked vacant lot across from Tom's grocery store with the same wide-open kind of hopeful energy. For a dollar in the Hoxie's sideshow you could see the Bearded Lady. For a five to get into the Waterfront Dance Club, you might very well meet the love of your life. And it seemed to me these were comparable thrills, adjusting for age and the rate of inflation.

Naomi put her elbows on her knees and smoked. The crowd on the Wharf was always moving, going nowhere. It grew neither bigger nor smaller like the patterns of colored glass in a kaleidoscope, only its shape changed when I looked at the water and then back again. The number of people who left the parking lot at the base of the Wharf seemed to be exactly replaced by the people coming back to get their cars. It was a little cross-section of white middle-class America laid out in the sun for my examination: thick-necked daddies with their milquetoast wives and slobbering progeny, young Bruce Springsteens and their Camero-haired girlfriends, born to run; platinum blondes in Queer Nation T-shirts and South Jersey accents holding hands with leather biker babes. And gay men in boots and hats and dresses. They cruised each other, walking up and down the street at the end of the Wharf like housewives check out supermarket produce; their eyes put back what they didn't want. Turn your head for a minute and their faces would get lost again in the crowd. Look away and back, and something else would have reached out to catch your eye.

At the end of the pier near the square in the street there was a tall, leggy woman. She was the first black face I'd seen all day that wasn't busing tables or sweeping floors. It was a comfort. The white girl beside her was nothing to look at but she had her own kind of stage presence. The white girl pulled me back to her when my eyes began to wander, the way your finger always seems to wind up in your best composed snapshots.

What it was with the white girl was her hair; it looked just like she'd escaped from a United States Marine Corps barber shaving new recruits. Soft, flabby recruits just out of street clothes. The contours of her body sloped down and out, her shoulders and chest settled at her waist like an inner tube from a truck tire. A five o'clock shadow of stubble on the sides of her head gave way to a swatch of red-brown hair slicked down the middle like a kind of tamed Mohawk. It made me glad no one had ever thought to do anything quite so au courant to my hair, but she didn't seem to mind.

The Marine recruit slipped her hand around the black girl's waist, dropped it down to the seat of her girlfriend's lycra shorts and then squeezed her ass as if she were staking a claim. I held my breath and waited for some right wing nut to shoot the Marine recruit dead in action, payment for her sexual audacity and not a little reward for the haircut. I was watching for the crowd to go belly to the pavement, but no one really seemed to care that the Marine recruit and her girlfriend were two girls who looked like Mutt and Jeff; and I wondered if Emily and I would have turned out any different if we'd had the guts to walk through the Chicago Loop holding hands.

VIII

The next morning I knew I had slept on my face; I had the sheet marks running across my cheeks to show for it, and all of my eyelashes were flattened down. I wet my fingers and tried to smooth them all in one direction, but my lashes were irreparably bent. Just my kind of hard luck on our first full day in the lesbian pick-up capital of the world. Of course, the sheet marks were just for starters.

I hadn't slept much, as Naomi had been kicking and calling hogs all night in the narrow Victorian bed, and the procession of comings and goings in the room next door had seemed nearly endless. There were circles under my eyes and the truth of it was, I was getting old. I was close to thirty. My skin didn't bounce back from everyday traumas the way it used to, and the circles and the sheet marks were the beginning of the end. And the end of Naomi's youth might be one thing, but the end of my own was a much more serious proposition.

I wasn't what you'd call a beautiful girl (though I had my moments when the light was low), and I was getting a little too old for cute, headed for the uncharted territory of middle-aged singleness. I had gotten used to marking the passage of years by the jewelry Emily bought me on our past four anniversaries. Now, I wondered how I would remember them in the future. Our relationship represented a large chunk of my life; it was a lot to let go of particularly when my body seemed to be falling apart. But like Naomi said, there was no sense throwing good commitment after bad.

Naomi had had a lot to say about relationships and commitment lately. Had it only been my own trouble, she wouldn't have cared. But Naomi and I were adversity-bonding now that Naomi had been dumped, too, by her ex-lover, Louise, a Gold Coast matron with a rich husband and time on her hands. Louise had left Naomi for a twenty-six-year-old tennis pro at their downtown club who looked like six creamy feet of Doris Day. Louise said the girl brought back her youth, a kind of *Pillow Talk* retrospective of the less complicated 1950s. Naomi said the only thing uncomplicated were Louise's flat-line brain waves. But I chalked it up to sour grapes. What was eating Naomi was that Louise had simply grown tired of her, impersonally, the way you might get sick of tuna fish salad for lunch. Of course, she recognized that to Louise she had always just been something different to do; what was hurting Naomi was that Louise had found something she thought was better. What was hurting me was that Emily had left me after four years together over what I thought was nothing, and for no one at all.

There seems to be an irresistible force that causes my relationships to self-destruct after a prescribed number of years. A kind of a Siren song that makes me want to hurl myself over the precipice into infidelities and deceit. I hadn't had the forethought to strap myself to the mast like Ulysses when I saw those Sirens coming this time and I was paying for it now.

What had made them sing to me? Maybe it was the lack of wedding china. Or the Christmases Em and I had spent, both of us well past the age of majority, at the homes of our respective parents rather than our own. I was ready to entertain the thought that relationships weren't supposed to last anymore, that there was a conspiracy of planned obsolescence like disposable cameras and automobile transmissions. My parents had been married thirty years; and I was ready to believe they just didn't make things like they used to.

That morning, Naomi had locked herself in the bathroom and the hot water ran relentlessly. She believed the steam was good for her complexion. Naomi could well have gone on like this for hours, despite the notice over the john asking guests to conserve water. But I didn't wait around to see.

Downstairs the parlor was empty and quiet, but the door to Sam's apartment was open. She was beating eggs for a souffle with a metal whip and the muscles in her upper arm stood out as she worked. She wore a pair of loud, loose-fitting cotton pants with a drawstring waist and the old canvas boating shoes I'd seen the day before. The print of her pants looked bright and happy, and Sam looked like a woman who liked to cook, really cook, not from mixes or out of packages, but someone who could turn flour and water into something. It was a nice thought if only in light of my own inability to make something concrete from more temperamental ingredients.

"I hope you don't mind my joining you," I said, "but Naomi's upstairs primping and I don't want to watch."

I thought the remark was clever and Sam smiled. She gave either my question or Naomi's primping some consideration. "Usually, I don't like people back here, but I guess it's all right." She held the mixing bowl between her chest and the crook of her arm and she was still turning the whip with a vengeance. "When you live with so many other women on season, you get to like your privacy."

I pulled a straight-back chair away from the table and sat with my legs tucked up around my chest. It was the way I always used to sit when I was a girl, waiting for my mother to let me lick the beaters from her Kitchenmaid mixer. My eyes ran along Sam's flowered wallpaper and I remembered my mother's lemon yellow kitchen.

This room and hall were all of the apartment I could see from where I sat. The kitchen was longish, with clean butcher block counters and European cabinets. Beside the back door was a corkboard with hooks on it where the keys for the rooms hung by their numbers. If I strained I could see the doors down the hall, but they were closed and I didn't much expect that Sam would like it if I gave myself a tour. But it tickled me a little that she kept the only break in the Victorian decor exclusively for herself. Even impeccable taste can get old. "Can I ask if there's a story behind all of this?" I said.

Sam said, "You can if you want. But it's a pretty long story about this house."

I looked down at my watch and told her I had all the time in the world.

Sam set the timer above the stove and closed the oven door on her souffle. "Well, I only have twenty minutes until this is done. If you want to hear about this house in twenty minutes, all right." Then she pulled a chair around for herself at a friendly distance and started talking.

The house was built in the early 1800s by a whaling captain for his new wife. Most everything in P-town had been built on money from whaling, Sam said — whaling and lately the charisma of successful artists mixed up with summer tourist dollars. When Sam had bought the house five years ago, it had belonged to a local attorney. When he retired, he and his wife had run it half-heartedly in the summers as a guest house, but he'd lost his heart for the business when his wife died. The attorney had up and moved to Florida. There were grown children, two girls living out of state with families of their own who didn't want the house which had gone downhill so badly since the old couple had abandoned it.

When Sam first saw the house, it needed paint and she didn't know what else, but she was taken with it in a way she couldn't explain to either her lover at the time or the real estate agent. She felt like she was coming home. She'd closed on it by the end of the month.

Sam told me, "You wouldn't believe how much work this place needed. But I was looking for a project and it took me and Anne five years to remodel it all." She closed her eyes. "We did the plumbing, the heat, the electrical, everything, and we ate macaroni and cheese some winters to make ends meet, but we loved each other and we loved this place. It's beautiful now and there's nothing left to do." Sam leaned back and rocked the kitchen chair on its rear legs. "It's kind of a letdown, you know?"

I was wondering mostly about Anne who clearly was no longer in residence, but I asked instead if Lavender House was full-up that week.

Sam pulled herself up in her chest like she was getting ready to brag. "I'm booked through most of the season already," she said. "I've got five rooms and I'm almost always full. My customers repeat. Two women should have got in last night. They come for a week every season. What's-their-names." She scratched the crown of her head and went on without remembering, "You'll see them at breakfast. They're nice girls. I had another cancellation

31

yesterday but it's pre-paid. And another couple checked in yesterday before you did, but you won't meet them this morning, they keep to themselves. I'll serve their breakfast later in their room."

"I thought you liked to get to know your guests," I said.

Sam grinned. "They're repeats. The room service is a special favor. Women like to stay here — I accommodate them. Sometimes women who can't stay the whole week pay me for it anyway just to reserve the room. I'm not complaining. You could rent a room on whatever terms you want down the road at Amelia's but you wouldn't be happy, I'll promise you that. Amelia would give up both her eye-teeth to have the kind of loyalty I get from my guests, but I've earned it." Sam said, "Half a dozen people own this whole town. You need a special entree or business sense like nobody's business to get a foot in the door."

I asked her which one she had and she laughed.

Sam told me she didn't get the letter of introduction when she took over. "But I've got the business sense. Years ago when these men bought up these guest houses, property was cheap, rates were cheap. They could stay half-empty all summer, the men could close them up for the winter and follow the sun to Greece. Women bought in later and paid more. I'm no exception. I stay open all year around because I have to and I'm lucky I can. Lavender House is in demand and I'll tell you it takes some hustle to cover this mortgage."

I said I didn't doubt it. "But that's only four

rooms rented," I said. "I thought you said you were booked up."

"I keep one room open usually." Sam shrugged and looked at her watch. "My house, my prerogatives."

The timer on the souffle went off and she got up from the table. "You'll have to excuse me now." She opened the oven door and held the souffle dish up like a trophy. A head of steam came off the dish. It was high and perfect and she was grinning at me as if she had just given birth.

IX

A little while after Sam had closed her apartment door behind me, the tall black woman I had seen on the MacMillian Wharf with the Marine recruit opened it up again. She walked in like she was a Las Vegas floor show and you were lucky if you got tickets. I thought she might be right. She had that leggy, high-breasted look that would make her a wonder at forty when everybody else's equipment had fallen. Besides being way too young for me, there was nothing wrong with her, but she was the kind of woman who would have to grow into her looks with age. Right then, at what I guessed to be maybe twenty-one, nature had given her a little too much to work with and she carried herself like she didn't quite know what to do with it all.

Her hair was pulled back off her face in a mane that ended up below her shoulders and the light brown fuzz at her temples was oiled within an inch of its life. She smelled faintly sweet, like hair being ironed at the kitchen table or like Sunday school at the African Methodist Episcopal Church; and she ran her hands through the back of her hair as fondly as if she were remembering past lovers. If she was, they were pleasant memories, not worth disturbing on my account, and she introduced herself as an afterthought when she had finished setting up the table.

"I'm Anya Pendleton." Anya looked like her entire body had been air-brushed. "I work on season helping Sam here at the guest house." She pulled her oversized blouse back onto her chocolate shoulder and twisted the little gold chain on her neck around her fingers. She told me, "I'm planning to go to journalism school when I graduate from college next year, but I think it's important to support exclusively women's places." There was space at the end of her sentence for a political discussion, but I let it slide.

She'd given me her politics and her prospects to let me know she had something else going besides this maid's job, to set herself apart in some way, besides her accent, from the kitchen/backroom Jamaicans who worked the Cape in the summers and occupied the eight-by-ten spaces for rent in local houses too dilapidated for tourists. That was all right. There was an envelope requesting tips for "the helper" which Sam had placed beside the vase of fresh flowers in their room, and I couldn't blame Anya for wanting to seem different from the summer migrant labor to a house full of rich white women.

What I couldn't figure out was what had convinced her she ought to be scrubbing toilets in aid of the revolution instead of putting in face-time as a lesbian feminist recruiting poster. If she liked the white feminist patter, the word I had was that women of color were in short supply and I thought Anya surely had the looks for high visibility. But mostly, I thought it was none of my business. She was nice enough scenery that I knew better than to look a gift horse in the mouth. I was thankful to see another brown face where I hadn't expected to find one. Anya Pendleton left me as warmed up and toasty as a cup of hot chocolate after a cold walk in the heavy snow. She let her chain drop back down the cleavage of her blouse without meaning anything by it and walked off to the kitchen like a runway model.

I sat back down again and some white women came in a while after I'd heard them coming down the stairs. The short-haired one poured them each a cup of coffee from the pot Anya had left on the buffet and closed her eyes while she drank hers. The other one swallowed hard and grunted. She sat down next to me with her coffee cup balanced on her knees and put out her hand for me to shake. Her friend stood by the buffet looking friendly enough.

The one who had shaken my hand said that her name was Barb. She had the kind of voice that carried even when it wasn't raised and she took my hand like she was used to working with stevedores. She and her friend were from Vermont, she said; the one with the short hair was called Jane.

"Chicago is a long way to come," Jane, the short hair said. Her face glowed with either youth or too much sun and I would have picked sun judging from the lines around her eyes.

I said, "I just hope it's worth it."

"Oh, it'll be worth it," said the loud one, Barb, "Believe me." She bobbed her head. We all nodded together like those sad-eyed dogs with springs for necks that people used to put in their windows when I was a kid. I hoped so.

"It'll be worth it," Barb said again. Then she turned to the quiet one and they both shook their heads in a togetherness like things that come in a set. "Oh, we love it here," the loud woman said.

Things had gone on in that vein for some time when Naomi came in from the porch. Anya was putting the food on the table and Sam directed the effort from the kitchen. Naomi took the seat across from me by the quiet woman and introduced herself.

"This is our favorite B and B and it's all because of Sam," said Barb. She got up to pour herself another cup of coffee from the buffet. She was saying, "Now, do you folks know Sam already? Well, we just love her. So will you when you get to know her like we do."

"Naomi knows Sam already," I said. The women from Vermont were getting on my nerves. They were the kind of women who believe that people and places begin to exist when they find out about them.

"Oh?" the quiet woman said to Naomi. "Have you been here before?"

"No." Naomi set her Marlboros down by her fork. "I just know Sam. That's all."

"No, I didn't think you'd been here before." Loud Barb looked down at the cigarettes. "Now that's a nasty habit." Food was caked all over her tongue. "We haven't seen you here and I've got quite a memory for faces."

The quiet woman nodded. Yes, the loud one, her Barb, could remember a face.

"So how do you know Sam?" Loud Barb asked. "I just love those kinds of stories. The world is so amazingly small, if you think about it." She paused for a moment, thinking about it.

Naomi spooned some sugar into her coffee. She blew over the cup and swallowed hard before she answered. "I used to sleep with her," she said, "as a matter of fact." She took another sip of her coffee and put her cup back down again as if she thought that was going to settle things. It didn't.

"Is that so," the loud woman said. "Well it's a small world." Nothing else seemed to occur to her. She laid her fork across the side of her plate and looked around the table smiling. "Small world," she said again.

Naomi took up her coffee cup and put it down again without drinking. "It was a long time ago," she said in a way that seemed calculated to suggest poor judgment. "And I was drunk — the first time anyway. I'd just like to let it die, if you don't mind." She clenched her teeth. She bit down on her tongue and looked genuinely wounded.

"Oh, well, I didn't mean anything by it," the loud woman, Barb, said to her friend. The quiet woman patted her hand like it was a kitten. "She oughtn't get so touchy," Loud Barb said.

Sam looked pretty touchy too. The muscles in her jaw were jumping against the side of her face like boiling water; she was red from the chest up. "I'd like it, Naomi, if you wouldn't indulge in revisionist history," said Sam. "It's news to me if I didn't suit you. You sure didn't tell me about it."

"I thought I'd call a spade a spade for once," Naomi said. Sam looked away after that and everybody was the soul of politeness all around.

"Well, well, Chicago is a long way away," Loud Barb said. "I travel a lot, but I don't get to Chicago much. It gets pretty hot there in the summer, huh?" She balled up her napkin by the side of her plate. Then she picked it up again and wiped her mouth. "Well." Loud Barb could stand the lull no more and began to share her opinions on baseball. She had worked her way through the minors before anyone noticed Joan Di Maio was standing in the doorway.

Joan was leaning on the door frame with one leg crossed behind the other. The pose effected the kind of a bad girl attitude I liked and the angry bruise below the roll of her denim shorts was backing it up. The bruise looked like a battle scar from a political demonstration and I thought I just might be in love. Joan made herself at home on the couch and hung her aviator sunglasses on the collar of her tank top. The thing about Joan was she looked like Emily, but bigger and butchier and I decided my attraction to women like this was a character flaw.

"I know Sam, and Anya," said Joan, "but I'm afraid everybody else is new." She smiled at me as if her lips were used to saying things like: harder, faster, and yes that's right. They were pink and taut and mildly leering on the kind of face that sells blue jeans and cigarettes.

"Joan's a writer," Sam said by way of introductions. "She was here with me a while ago to do a story on hate crimes when a gay man got beat up in Dennisport."

Then Sam got up from the table and sat so close to Joan on the couch that their thighs were pressed together. Sam's voice was full of pride and covet. "Joan's been staying in the room right next to yours, Virginia, while she's working on a history of Provincetown."

Loud Barb asked if she was a historical writer and Joan smiled as though her primary emotion was self-satisfaction. "Not usually. It's a gay history."

"You don't say." Loud Barb shared that she had once written what everyone at U Mass had said was a fine article for a college paper on the rise of roller derby in the northeast. "I read a piece about Gay Studies in *The Rolling Stone*," Loud Barb said. "Are you some kind of an academic?"

Sam laughed and she let her hand come to rest on the ball of Joan's knee. "Oh no. Joan's a newspaper writer. She writes a syndicated column for Gay and Lesbian papers all over the country."

"*Outtime*," said Anya.

Outtime was like a lesbian ramble with Paul Harvey, in hard copy. I'd read it myself. Joan Di Maio, whose name was sounding a lot more familiar now that someone had mentioned her column, was like the Roving Reporter. She made it her business to sniff out controversy involving the Gay and Lesbian community and then jump right into the middle of it, exposing hypocrisy in your government or right in your own back yard, naming names or threatening to. Joan set herself up as judge and jury and then she printed the transcripts of the trial without inviting the accused to participate. She called it "Justifiable Outting," pulling closeted queers out of their closets sometimes for crimes against the gay community, sometimes because they were famous and closeted, sometimes just because they were closeted. I thought the McCarthy-style hysteria of her politics made better theater than serious journalism. But her columns had that grocery-store check-out line emotional pitch that made them both tantalizing and scary to people like me who worked at straight jobs. Sure, it was great to know my favorite blonde-haired screen actress was queer as a three-dollar bill, but we little nameless cogs in the great societal gear box were always a little nervous over the possibility that this kind of notice might be directed at us personally. I wasn't sure it would improve my employment prospects if my sexual orientation became a topic for lunchroom gossip at Whytebread and Grease, the investment firm where I was hell bent on making partner. The rumors hadn't hurt the re-election campaigns of rich, established white male senators much, but somehow I didn't think I needed to advertise my membership in yet another downtrodden minority group.

I felt better reading about Joan's triumphs over hypocrisy and evil from far away, but it didn't cut down on her celebrity appeal. The aura of dyke fame seemed to be making Anya a little breathless too. She tossed her hair, and her hoop earrings jingled attractively against her face as she cleared the table.

She was killing herself to catch Joan's eye across the room. I watched her lips make the words in something less than a whisper and twice as urgent. She was saying, "I need to talk to you. Now." It was taking all of her concentration and she didn't care that I was watching her. When the whispering didn't work, Anya stuck out her lip and stacked the dirty plates inside each other very loudly.

"How exciting," the quiet woman was saying to Joan. "We're just thrilled. I've always said I was going to write a book. Didn't I, Barb?" She slapped the loud one on the knee. "You must tell us how you did your research and when your book is going to be published."

Loud Barb grunted like she wanted Joan to go away.

"I'd love to tell you all about it sometime." Joan wrinkled up her eyes.

"Would you really?" the quiet one said. "You'll have to promise. Won't that be exciting, Barb?" Loud Barb crossed her arms and grunted some more.

"I'm less of a writer and more of an activist really," Joan was saying. "I like to think of myself as a guerilla warrior for gay and lesbian rights." From my reading of her columns, I thought that fit. The quiet woman, Jane, was impressed to silence by this commitment, but I thought the jury was still out.

"I'm in accounting myself," Loud Barb said.

Joan pursed her lips like she had tasted something sour. "We all have to do what's best for us."

"Well, it's big eight at least." Barb counted on her fingers. "Well, big six now."

41

"There have been some mergers recently," the quiet woman explained.

"I hadn't known," said Joan.

Anya dropped the stack of dirty dishes on the table top, but nothing sounded broken. Then she went off slamming the door to the kitchen. Sam followed her, frowning, and I watched Naomi's eyes go along with Sam. Her head didn't move, but for a second she wore an expression I'd seen on her face sometimes when she and Louise were new, a look of amusement just short of a smile. It was a look I was glad to see again.

"Well," the loud woman giggled. "What's that they say about 'good help?' "

I didn't like her tone enough to do something about it. "I wouldn't know what they say about the help," I said.

"Well," said Loud Barb. "Well, no offense. It's a sad day when people can't take a little joke."

I was going to tell her I thought she was a joke when Naomi said, "I think the Cubs might go all the way this year," and the loud woman took long-winded exception to that kind of thinking.

The Cubs didn't thrill me, so I poured myself a cup of tea and went over to check out Joan on the couch. It was curiosity mostly, wondering whether Joan was really worth a cat fight between Sam and Anya. But somebody thought she was worth quite a lot; there was an emerald-cut diamond that looked like estate jewelry on her left hand. It didn't go with the blonde butch attitude she was throwing off, so I figured it was a gift. And I had a pretty good idea where it had come from.

"You're staying here at Lavender House." Maybe

42

I meant it as an ice-breaker, maybe not, but Joan took it as an open invitation.

She said, "For a while." Joan laid her ankle across her knee. "I gather we're neighbors, then." She was wearing combat boots over white crew socks. She had pretty good legs and she knew it. "I work best at night; I hope you'll let me know if I'm keeping you up. And if ever you find you can't sleep, please knock on my door." Her teeth were sharp and even, and she showed them a lot. She was the kind of woman who didn't like to be alone and knew ways to avoid it. Joan said, "I keep a bottle of gin for late nights and I've been known to share."

"I'll remember that." She had the kind of looks that grow on you and eyes so much like a warm bath, I thought I might need a cold shower.

Loud Barb was holding forth on slow-pitch softball now.

"How long are you staying?" Joan managed to make it sound like my itinerary really mattered to her.

I told her we were leaving a week from the following Wednesday and she smiled like it was timing she could work with. Then she sized up Naomi. She was taking inventory of the women in the room the way Andrew Jackson looked at Florida in 1812. I could see right through her but it didn't matter. Joan leaned back on the couch with her hands above her head and raised her voice for Sam's benefit. "I haven't decided yet how long I'm here for. As long as Sam can put up with me, I guess." She winked at Sam who it seemed to me was never very far away.

"I was team captain of the women's softball team

at my firm four years in a row," Loud Barb was saying and she turned to the quiet one who jerked her head up and down. Barb was so happy to be reminded of the championship she seemed not to care that Sam had turned her attention back to Joan, and that Naomi had sneaked off for a smoke on the porch. I watched her chatter to her girlfriend at the dining table across the room, but her voice had dropped down low. Every once in a while, the quiet one would giggle and slap her on the knee.

Sam was standing next to me, wiping her hands on her apron. "I gave Anya the rest of the day off, poor kid. She's not feeling well all of a sudden and I can manage today by myself." Sam sat down on the couch between me and Joan. She was smiling so thinly that I thought I might scratch the good humor off her face if I wasn't careful and I didn't want to see what was underneath it.

"I hope our Joan is entertaining you." Sam looked like her hope was just the opposite and I didn't think it was prudent to answer.

Joan's palm cupped around Sam's knee as if her hand had been there before and often. "Honey, I had the oddest dream last night," she said. "I dreamed there were cats jumping on my bed, throwing sand all around. When I woke up there was sand in my sheets."

"Were they like the picture in your room? Long-haired cats?" Sam's cheeks were red; her voice was high and excited. "Like the Victorian lady in a blue dress on the couch with the cats?"

Joan looked attractively blank and stupid as if details were escaping her. "Sure," she said, "like that."

"I got her last season at a rummage sale in Truro, the lady in the picture, and funny things have been happening in that room ever since. I'm not joking. I call her the Lady in Blue." Sam wagged her finger. "Don't you laugh, Joan. I've had to move a lot of women out of that room because she spooks people. Some women have taken her right off the wall. I'll find her under the bed sometimes or wrapped up in blankets in the closet after they've left. I'll see a blue flash out of the corner of my eye when I'm up there alone cleaning sometimes and I know it's her."

"Do you think this place is haunted?" Joan offered to call her publisher in Tallahassee. "I'm sure she'd buy a gay ghost story as long as it had some sex. It might sell even better than a gay history of Provincetown."

"No, I wouldn't say haunted," Sam said. "I think haunted might be a little strong, but I've had women here with allergies to cats who've complained about that room. I've had to move them PDQ."

"Well, I've never had any problems with cats." Joan looked at me as if Sam were a little crazy and I found myself thinking the same. Joan's eyes on mine made me feel as if I ought to blush.

"Don't you laugh at me." Sam shook her finger at Joan some more and said, "You'll be sorry later when you see I'm right."

Joan said she thought she already was. "If I have any problems tonight, I'll be sure to call." She laid her hand on Sam's thigh as if it were her own and I felt like we were three-on-a-date.

"I guess Naomi and I should get to the beach if we're going." I told her I was sorry about the scene at breakfast. "Naomi can be funny sometimes," I said.

"Oh, I know, Naomi." Sam stood up from the couch. "I'd better get back to work, if Anya's going to be off." Joan followed her close carrying the dirty dishes from breakfast as if she knew how to bus tables. She found the extra hand to close the door to Sam's apartment behind her.

X

The Provincetown police station was a friendly white frame building with grey shingled sides and a little red brick porch with an iron railing that ran along its edge. It looked more like somebody's house than an official location, but I was still pretty happy to leave it.

The sheriff guided me by the crook of my elbow the way you help bent old ladies cross the street. He escorted me out of the building, down the red brick steps and to the curb of the circular driveway, but I didn't feel particularly comforted by his special attention. He opened the back door of the patrol car and held it open like a gentleman, but somehow it didn't feel much like a courtesy.

"The deputy will drive you back over to Lavender House." He said it as if he was doing me a favor but he let his hand rest on the door handle until I got in, so I knew I didn't have much choice of how I was going back to the guest house. "I can't order you of course," he said, "but we'd appreciate it if you'd stay close by." He closed the car door and stepped back to the curb. I watched him through the back window of the squad car. He was furrowing up his eyebrows at me as the deputy pulled away.

The ride back to Lavender House was silent as the grave; and the deputy let me open the car door myself, but he waited until I got onto the porch before he backed out of the driveway. I could feel him watching me shut the guest house door.

No one was in the parlor when I came in. The Lavender House was quiet and I was glad for the privacy. I had chosen not to cry in front of Harmon; I thought he would have liked to see my tears. But when I closed the guest house door behind me, I felt the water come on and sometimes you can only hold things in for so long before they have to see the light of day. I stood in the parlor and cried, then, without restraint, until I couldn't catch my breath in the heaving, sobbing way of children.

But for all of my histrionics, it was odd to know that I hadn't even liked Joan much, although, I couldn't deny I'd wanted to sleep with her. And it made me sick to think I might be crying over the space she'd left in my fantasy life instead of the place she now occupied in my own private lesbian chamber of horrors. It made me sick to be crying over missing closure. But I couldn't stop.

I'd started with Joan but I finished with things I'd wanted to cry about before like Em and Susan and a friend I'd lost named Beverly Johnson in a story that was too long to repeat and too sad to remember very often. And whether or not I was watering the ground on Joan's behalf, the tears felt genuine enough and I always felt better after a cry. This time was no exception.

I blew my nose at my reflection in the oak framed mirror over the buffet. The glass was warped. It bent my face, all streaked and stained like hard water marks on Victorian plumbing. My neck was sweating like an old grey pipe and my arms were cool and covered with goose bumps. I closed my eyes and felt the goose bumps with my hands.

My reflection wiped her nose on the sleeve of her sweatshirt and I thought it would have been nice to have some breakfast. Or lunch. My watch said 11:30, Wednesday, and I was out of luck in more ways than one. The police had come and gone and the box of donuts they'd left on the buffet was empty except for sticky pieces of donut paper.

I took a magazine from the rack beside the claw foot reading chair and settled on the couch. I didn't feel like reading, but I felt much less like thinking, at least not about the last four hours of my life, and I could hear my stomach complaining in memory of last night's meal.

Three blocks from the ocean Lavender House still smelled like salt and furniture oil. The smell of salt could always make me hungry; it took me back nearly twenty years to when my father paid my bills and I didn't appreciate how little ugliness there was in my life.

Summer in Delaware always smelled like mold and damp sea air to me. The wood frame of the house never dried out and silverfish hid in the dark wet corners of the deck, under the chair where my father read the newspapers.

My father went out every morning before we woke up to buy the *New York Times* and the regional rags. He set them in a stack beside his wooden chair on the deck before breakfast. After we ate, he'd turn the deck chair out of the sun and read his papers in the shade, looking up from the print to wave when my mother took us off to the beach, then looking down again before we were gone. When we came home in the afternoons, my father would not seem to have moved from where we'd left him that morning, but he'd have worked his way through the stack of newspapers, and his chair would be turned to follow the shade. My father would be sleeping with his ankles crossed and his bare feet up on the wooden ottoman. A paper would lie open on his chest and when my mother shook him he would claim to have only been resting his eyes. He'd stretch as if his knees were stiff and then, later, drive us down the highway for crab cakes.

I hadn't remembered the good parts of those summers for a long time. And I would have liked to put my feet up and think about them some more, but Sam's antiques seemed too delicate; they put me off my usual habits. The couch where I sat was a wooden-legged, dainty affair but the embroidered upholstery gave in easily to the weight of my hips. Its pillows rose up in a homey way to meet my lower back and I could not really complain.

The guest house parlor was a comfortable room on the whole. Like the rest of the house it brooded, filled with porcelain curios and heavy furniture, dark wood and cane. The sun came in streaks through the deep bay windows by the table, but near the foyer where I sat it was dark and cool, and the breeze flapped the long lace curtains out into the room. Thinking of Joan, I looked down at the arm of the couch and couldn't stop my hand from shaking.

XI

Herring Cove beach is a blistering forty-minute walk from Lavender House in the sun, down Bradford Street past the gas station, past the one-level drive-up tourist motels, and on to Route Six-A where the sidewalk ends. There is a bus that rides back and forth down Bradford between the center of town and the beach. The fare is one dollar. If you drive, admission to Herring Cove is five bucks per car. Or you can buy an annual Cape Cod National Seashore pass for fifteen dollars that's good all summer.

My second day in Provincetown, Sunday, when Naomi and I came over the dunes by the parking lot, there was nothing to see for it seemed like miles of dirty sand and white girls oiled with drugstore suntan lotion. The crowd had segregated itself more or less into gays and lesbians, and straights and gays. The lesbians were near the parking lot where the trail came out of the dunes as if they had dropped their beach equipment the minute they saw water; the gay men were a little ways south, towards Wood End Lighthouse with a preference for privacy; and the straights both male and female were camped out north past the boathouse and the concession stand towards Race Point and a second parking lot. At the boundaries, the lines of separation blurred and the various groups looked across the beach at one another with confusion and amusement, the way you would thumb through the issues of *National Geographic* when you were a kid.

In the distance, the water was blue and cold as February. The heat bent the air above the sand and two identical-looking, balding white businessmen in sun bonnets with pink ballerina netting wrapped around the brims skipped across the beach. Everybody clapped; the sisters in the hats waved and bowed to their lesbian public, and all around us there were girls. All shapes and sizes and grades of vanilla. Some few black ones were mixed in like chocolate chips in a dish of premium ice cream.

I watched the women run from the beach straight into the ocean and dunk down all at once so as not to lose their nerve. They came up gasping, and pressed the water out of their hair as they got lost again in the warmer sea of women on the beach. And the park rangers sneaked along behind the dunes in little carts that looked like riding-style lawn mowers, ready to ticket any woman with her breasts exposed; the topless dykes flipped themselves defensively whenever anyone shouted, "Ranger!"

The women we'd met on the highway had their volleyball net flying like a flag near where the gay men sat. They had come prepared with deck chairs and beach umbrellas and one big red metal cooler. From their portable radio Melissa Etheridge was wailing some sad song of failed conquest. I spread our blanket out by the dunes where the sand was cleaner, took a beer from our little cooler bag and popped the top. We were close enough to have a look at the girls from New Jersey, and far enough away not to notice them if some better opportunity came along.

"What's the problem with you and Sam anyway," I said to Naomi. She had already lit up a Marlboro where she lay at the other end of the blanket. Her eyes were closed and I watched her face over the top of my beer can. "I don't like to be embarrassed," I said.

Naomi sighed. She let the leftover smoke drift out of her mouth. "Old wounds, I guess." She put her sunglasses on and looked out at the water instead of me. The corners of her mouth slumped down and she sighed again like she was tired. She said, "I don't see how you were embarrassed."

I told her Sam must have hurt her pretty badly and I set my beer down beside the towel like I wanted to listen, but Naomi wasn't talking very much.

"Don't be sorry. I was the one who hurt her anyway." Naomi shrugged. "Not the other way around. Put some oil on my back, will you?" She put her cigarette out in the sand. "I want to get really dark, all right?"

On the towel next to us was a topless woman with olympic tits reading *Tales of the City* and I would have liked to hear Naomi's story, but I figured the view was better than nothing. I told the woman with the tits that her book looked good and she caught my meaning. She had red lipstick and cats-eye glasses so dark I couldn't see her eyes.

"Have you read it?" she said. I hadn't and she asked if I wanted to. I thought it was gratifying that after four years out of circulation I hadn't forgotten how to flirt.

"Will you hold off the oil, Virginia," Naomi was complaining and the woman on the towel turned back to her book with a look of complete self-satisfaction.

Naomi said, "What would you do with a thirty-six-year-old woman who couldn't manage to keep a regular relationship?"

"I'd introduce her to you, Naomi." I pinched her leg. "But you're a little older than that, aren't you?"

"Fuck you," said Naomi. She lit another cigarette and blew the smoke out hard over her head.

Down the beach, the girl who had fixed the car was trying to start a volleyball game. She tossed the ball up every so often and caught it again. She kicked the sand around with the toe of pink, high-top sneakers laced ice-skate style and tied in a double bow at her ankles by way of a fashion statement. The volleyball went up and down above her head. I watched her for a while, then got up and wiped the sand off the back of my shorts. "I'm going over there to talk to that girl from Route Six," I said. "But you can stay if you want."

Back over my shoulder Naomi was standing up. "Fuck you," she said again, but she followed me down the beach anyway.

"Hiya, babe," the car girl said when we got within shouting distance. "I guess you got here okay." She had the kind of voice that peoples Cadillacs with furry dice and after-hours bars in Queens, but her smile looked like a toothpaste ad.

"We got in fine," I said.

She said, "Oh, I can see that, babe. You want a beer?" She was drinking Lite and she held the can out to share. "So, where you girls from?" The car girl looked down at her shoes when she'd finished talking as if she'd suddenly remembered she was shy. Somehow I doubted it.

"We're from Chicago." I handed back the beer and Naomi looked down her nose at the can as if it had the plague.

The car girl nodded, one hand stuck in her pocket. "I know Chicago. I'm from New York myself, originally, the City, that is."

"Do you get there often," Naomi asked, "to Chicago," like she didn't care what the answer was.

The car girl looked at the ground again and shook her head. "I've never been to Chicago, actually, but I know where it is if that's what you mean." Then she looked sideways at me and smiled. "Maybe I'll get there sometime now."

"Maybe you will." I was smiling back. "We'd like that, huh, Naomi?" I said.

Naomi sat down in the car girl's empty deck chair and rolled her eyes. She fired up a Marlboro and let the smoke drift peacefully out of her Roman nose. Someone had told her once that this was sexy but I couldn't see it.

"So where are you from, anyhow?" the fat girl was saying to Naomi. "We're from Jersey except for Jo there," and she pointed at the car girl. "She's from New York City."

"Well, I'd like it anyway if you came to Chicago," I said. I was wondering what the car girl looked like without her clothes. I was wondering where her tan lines stopped and she smiled back at me from under her eyebrows as if she could tell what I was thinking.

"Is that your girlfriend?" The car girl nodded at Naomi and sounded like she wanted to offer condolences.

I shook my head. "How about you? Where's your girlfriend?"

The car girl looked down at the sand. She didn't want me to think that she was the kind of girl who would fuck around — at least not yet. But that, of course, was just the kind of girl she was. It was, of course, the kind of girl that I'd become — and we recognized each other.

"Actually, my girlfriend's back in the City right now. She had to work. I miss her, you know, actually," the car girl said. "So, you want another drink, babe?"

I didn't mind that the car girl hadn't covered her mouth to burp. She held her beer out again with the kind of charming shyness that evaporates in bed and I finished the better part of the can.

"I thought we were going to play volleyball," I said after a while. Some girls were taking sides around the net and the car girl gave me her slow smile again. But she volunteered for the other team and I should have taken it as a hint.

My team was sadly over-matched. We had a gym teacher in a black bikini the size of a postage stamp, but the other women were five slow-moving, wide-bodied girls and I knew we were going to have a problem when the gym teacher had to explain the rotation. She promised everybody that it was okay if we couldn't hit the ball and she looked around at the wide-bodied girls, then pointed to me. "Can you serve?" The gym teacher sounded a little desperate.

I said I could but it was a lie.

The gym teacher looked relieved. She tossed me the ball underhand. "You serve, then." She drew a line in the sand with her pink toenail and pulled her bikini down low over her butt like she was ready to get down to business.

I took the server's position in back of the line and looked across the net into the car girl's chest; none of the other team's girls were shorter than five foot-eight and none of them needed a refresher course on volleyball rotation.

We were hopeful, though. The wide-bodied girls were giving each other high fives. I served the ball the way I remembered from High School gym class, off my palm, with the usual results. It went straight into the net and I could hear Naomi laughing from her deck chair. The ball rolled back over my toes and I stared down at it for a while before I picked it up again and tossed it under the net.

The gym teacher sighed. Then she closed her

eyes. She took a deep, long breath and clapped her hands. "Good try," she said, "Good play. Now, let's get up for the next one, ladies."

It was a tall order. The other team's first server looked like white America's answer to Grace Jones. Grace served overhand like a tennis player and all of her serves stuck in the sand by the net where I and the wide-bodied girls had missed them one after another. Our gym teacher finally shoved me aside and dove for the last one. But we lost anyway, having never even been in the game, and I thought it was the story of my life.

The gym teacher blew her nose onto the ground sadly and clapped her hands some more. "Good game. Good game," she said to everybody and she walked off slowly shaking her head.

I followed the retreat of her low-riding bikini line along the beach with regret. The sun was beating down like a rhythm section and the only good reason I could think of for holding my eyelids open was to look at the car girl on the blanket beside me. I was making eyes and she was making eyes back, but after two beers in the heat even that couldn't keep me awake for long. I was almost out for the count when I felt somebody kick sand in my face and I looked up at Anya's Marine recruit standing over our blanket. Her feet were about a size nine and a half.

"Hey, you want to come see a show?" The Marine recruit talked like she was used to getting her way. She handed me a xeroxed flyer on pink paper from a stack she had tucked under her arm. "I'm Hillela Hill, the comic."

I read the flyer. Apparently she was. The picture had caught her laughing and her mouth was wide open like there was something irrepressibly funny going on. The hook was: she would let you in on it when you came to see her routine. Underneath the grainy xeroxed picture the caption said *Hillela Hill in her natural state.* Apparently this was mirth.

"So, you want to come see a show?" Hillela had a broad meaty face and her eyes caught the light like shiny buttons on an upholstered couch. She squinted down the beach, shading her eyes with her hand while she waited for me to answer.

"Aw fuck," said Hillela suddenly. She ran her hand over the razor stubble on the side of her head and made a face. "Will you just look at that." In the field of white girls nearby she had spotted Anya by the high water mark sitting with Joan on a beach towel the size of a cheap motel washcloth. Their heads were bent together and Joan was talking with her hands. Hillela pointed directly at them. "I tell you, this kind of shit can ruin your day." Whatever else she had to say was said so low in her throat that I couldn't hear the words. But I didn't imagine it was part of her act.

Hillela dropped the stack of flyers on the towel beside me. "Give these to your friends for me, will you? I've got to go or I'm going to kill somebody." As she stalked off towards the dunes, I could see that even if Hillela's natural state was a belly laugh, it was clearly subject to change.

Joan's skin had turned the color of boiled lobster and I could hear their conversation come over on the breeze and I listened to it for my own reasons.

"Monogamy limits us," Joan was saying.

Anya put her hand across her mouth and yawned

like she'd heard it before. "Right." She stretched her arms over her head and turned her flat, bare chest towards the sun.

The car girl woke up and started rubbing my back. Naomi was watching us with a disgust that I attributed to jealousy, and the woman with the curly hair continued to ignore her.

Joan was saying, "Don't you understand, that kind of exclusivity divides us. It closes us off to things."

"Right." Anya covered her mouth again with her palm and scrunched up her eyes. "What things do you mean?" she said. "Like sex with other people." It wasn't a question.

"That too." Joan smiled. "Why don't you let me rub your back."

"Did you know you have beautiful eyes," the car girl told me. "Did anyone ever tell you that?"

"Why don't you tell me about your friend who writes for the *New York Times*," Anya said to Joan.

"Fine," said Joan. "She works for the *New York Times*. Why don't you let me rub your back? I can tell you're tense. Our relationships are extensions of how we are in the world." Joan started working the muscles in Anya's back while she babbled out her politics. "You know monogamy shuts us off from possibilities. Oogamy, open. Monogamy, closed. Christ," Joan said. "Goddess, just listen to the sounds of the words and you can feel what they're telling you."

But Anya didn't look like she was listening. She didn't even look like she was enjoying the backrub much.

"You mean nobody's really ever told you that about your eyes?" the car girl asked again. "Actually?"

"Why don't you tell me about working for the *Tribune*," Anya said and Joan let her hands drift offsides to Anya's breasts like she was selling more than political dogma. "What was it like working for a big newspaper?" Anya said. Whatever Joan was selling, she wasn't buying it.

Joan pressed down on Anya's back with the heels of her hands and grunted. "I've told you already. It wasn't what you think it is." She was irritable when she didn't get her way. Joan said, "Mainstream journalism isn't really the pursuit of Truth and Beauty. The closest I've got to that is at the gay papers with my column. In mainstream journalism you don't get to write what you want and I quit because I couldn't condone the hypocrisy. Here we are journalists supposed to expose the truth and I brought my editor conclusive proof that one of the most anti-gay legislators in Springfield was queer. Illinois had just lost the state human rights legislation in part thanks to him and the *Trib* wouldn't even print the story. My editor said a man's sex life had nothing to do with his voting record. I asked him how a journalist could turn away from hypocrisy."

Apparently Joan always talked like a message from your local gay and lesbian political action committee — either that or Don Giovanni. Still, I would have liked to have the confidence it takes to quit a job because I didn't like my boss's politics. But then again, Joan's landlord was Sam and the rates looked pretty easy. For myself, I just wasn't able to conceptualize hopping into the sack with my account officer from Horizon Savings and Loan every time my mortgage came due or with the check-out girl at the Jewel Store every time I needed groceries. I might have considered the check-out girl under different circumstances, but that was what had gotten me into hot water with Em in the first place. I figured poor working stiffs like myself would just have to wait for the revolution to come and politicize our work places for us.

"You can't work against the community and remain protected by it." Joan was giving little karate chops to Anya's upper back. "It's all about power. White men want to have all the power for themselves. This is exactly what I've been trying to explain to you, Anya, about that education you're so proud of. It all comes down to power. Patriarchy, imperialism, racism, sexism. They're all the same. That's why they're fighting against inclusive education at every university in this country. The ruling classes want to homogenize and desex us. They argue that what is scholarly, what is important, is exclusively straight and white in genesis. If we want an education that tells the truth about women and gays and people of color in this country, we have to rewrite the book." Joan paused, her hands mid-chop on Anya's shoulders, and shook her. "Are you listening? We have got to re-educate ourselves or we're going nowhere."

Joan sighed. "You know, Anya, I'm concerned sometimes that you're a little too attached to the trappings of the existing white power structure." She sighed again and rubbed her hands along Anya's hips.

If someone had told me those hands had won a lot of political arguments, I wouldn't have been surprised. But I had to wonder whether Sam knew Joan had gotten so friendly with her helper.

"Do you mean to say no one has ever told you that stuff about your eyes?" the car girl said and up by the dunes some baby dykes were kissing.

XII

I saw the car girl again on Monday night at the Waterfront Dance Club. She was working her way back from the bar with her elbows. The place was wall-to-wall girls but the car girl's size made a place for us in the crowd. She held an armful of drinks like a professional barmaid. Her shirt was open and her chest was pale and flat with a tan line from the front of her tank suit.

"Oh babe," she said, "do you look good in clothes."

The music was loud and the car girl stood closer rather than shouting; I had to feel her breath to hear her.

"I mean you look good in clothes .. too," the car girl explained and I laughed like it was just the kind of thing I wanted to hear. It was.

"We have a table over there." She was selling

brown-eyed seduction and I was a sucker for it. Em had said it before, but she wouldn't have liked that she was right.

The curly-headed girl and her heavy friend were sitting by the wall near the dance floor and I followed the car girl through the crowd, pressing my palms on the shoulders of strangers and bumping up against the backs of chairs to get by. It was a friendly, hopeful crowd and women turned to smile at us as we passed.

"So, where's your friend?" the heavy girl asked when I got to the table.

I told her Naomi was still in the line at the bar trying to get our drinks. It was a rare fit of generosity and I hadn't wanted to distract her. I pointed.

"Well, let's get her over here." The fat girl laid her cigarette in the dirty glass ashtray and waved across the dance floor for Naomi. "Sit down, honey," she said to me. "You're making me tired."

The car girl took a drag on the heavy one's cigarette. She blew the smoke out over her head and put it back. I thought the car girl wore her habits well. She ran her fingers through her short dark hair. The air over the table was blue and the DJ started to play a slow set.

"Let's dance, okay?" The car girl had sized me up and she didn't wait for an answer.

"Your friend can keep the chair warm," the curly-headed girl said as if she thought I might have said no, and Naomi smirked because she knew me better.

"You crack me up," the heavy girl was saying to Naomi, "you know that?" Her entire girth rolled back and forth when she laughed. "You kill me." Her breasts jiggled on her belly. The curly-headed one smiled a closed mouth smile.

It was a long set and the car girl danced well, I thought, like the way she would fuck. She poured herself across the floor like she was made of warm molasses and she whispered half-thoughts to the ridges of my ear. I had no doubt that we would go to bed. The mystery that remained was how she would seduce me. I counted out the possibilities with each grind of her hips. She rocked me like a lullaby until she whispered that she was tired of dancing.

So, we drank on the deck behind the bar away from the others. I left my arms around her waist at the start of her hips and closed my eyes. Her kisses were full of spit and promise and her hands slid up the legs of my shorts.

"I wish you could come to New York and stay with my girlfriend and me," the car girl said as if the idea of three-way sex were something she'd just recently invented. It was a disappointment, when I had wished for some romantic remark to remember her by, a memento of the evening that I could rerun to feed my ego when Em walked out again and I felt lonely or unattractive. I had wanted to remember the car girl the way Loud Barb would remember her triumphs on the softball field when her joints were too brittle to play anymore. I had wanted adoration and the car girl could only offer up her lust. It would be, I thought, the worse for her.

"What would your girlfriend think about that?" I said and laughed as if it were a joke between us.

The car girl laughed too and didn't answer. She leaned against the rail of the deck, open-legged, and kissed me again with her lazy tongue lolling back behind my teeth.

High tide came in over the car girl's shoulder. The moon was full and it didn't matter to me that I didn't know the car girl's name. Who she was could not compare with my imagination. I was waiting to be caught up in that familiar flow of hope and lust that makes wonder from another woman's ordinary body. For me it was always like this, the re-invention of myself in first encounters. New lovers promise you a future, free from the boredom that poisons well-worn relationships and then they fade into the disappointing routine of long-haul commitment when your lover cannot stretch to be all the things you have imagined.

This is where Emily had failed me — in expectation. She was a house built of stone while I was built of wood and mud; I required maintenance and I wanted a love that is painted over into something else whenever it begins to fade. I wanted new additions. Em wanted only the confidence in my stone fidelity, an impossible thing for the weak of faith to give in a world that is full of temptation and so empty of moral support.

I don't fault myself. You can't control what you want and shouldn't be blamed for it. What I wanted was a woman as flexible as builder's putty to fill in the empty spaces in my life. I wanted a woman as large as a circus tent to wrap around me and keep me safe, as deep as the potholes in the city streets when the spring thaw comes, to make a home for me in the ugly world. Em could not bend and stretch like a tarp and I had not learned to live happily with the compromise.

And the car girl groaned in completion of less complicated goals. And when her friend, the heavy woman, found us on the deck, she wore a smile just like a dirty joke and said the bar was closing. She left. I watched her walk across the deck until the doorway where she had gone was dark again. And the car girl finished her beer in gulps. She took my hand and left her empty glass on the railing for the wind.

XIII

Out on the street there was a commotion by the benches in front of Town Hall. A man was screaming, "*Faggots!*" like breaking bottles against a concrete gutter. The sound fell out of his mouth as if he could both kill and cry, but didn't know which to do. His screaming stopped the people where they stood and called them close around him to hear more. It raised the fine "kitchen" of hair on the back of my neck and made a crowd like a puddle in the street to watch him screaming.

"*Faggots!*" His voice was loud and hard as a gunshot and he threw his arms up around his head.

The curly-headed girl took hold of the heavy one's arm. "He's drunk," she was saying. "He must be drunk to shout like that," she said as if she were asking a question.

"Of course he's drunk," the heavy girl said and the curly-headed one kept hold of her arm.

"I'll kill you faggots." His raised arms ended in the balls of his fists. "Touch me and I'll kill you bastards."

He would stand and scream; then fall to his knees and scream some more while people were saying that he must be drunk. There were other men standing not very near him, just out of reach of the lights mounted on the roof of the town building so that their faces were covered by shadows.

One of them said, "Go on home why don't you." And four or five other men spoke then, so softly that what they were saying was drowned out by the screaming, but the man who was down kept screaming anyway. The other men came closer and stood around him trying to talk sense to him but he wouldn't hear it.

"Fuckers," he said. "I'll kill you faggots."

Somebody in one of the guest houses fronting the street had called the police. Two policemen came after a while and took the man away still screaming. In the lights of their car he was only a little thin-hipped boy. He was drunk, and the blood ran out of his nose all down his shirt. He rubbed his nose with his fists, still crying and promising death to the men he said had hit him.

The men by the Town Hall told the police the boy had hit one of them first, a man with a shaved head and a hanging cross earring, for speaking to the boy as they passed in the street. The boy had offered to beat them all. The one with the shaved head had knocked him down and the boy had fallen on his face. Then the other ones tried to talk sense to him, but he'd hit the shaved head one again, and again had been knocked down.

The police shook their heads. They let the shaved head man go, and put the boy in the back of the car. He couldn't scream anymore and went easily. His voice was hoarse and sad the way a stuck horn gives up as the battery dies out.

The men watched the police car pull off down the street and then went on their way. People who had come out to watch went back behind their doors and the New York girls got in their car and drove off towards Herring Cove. Their headlights glowed in the unlit street like the last red coals at the end of a campfire.

XIV

July 20

Sometimes I wonder why it is I write to you when you won't ever read this. But it has seemed to me for a long time that we're connected you and I, as if we had taken two different roads just like that poem; you know the one. Do you know what will happen when our paths finally cross? It makes me smile.

XV

At one o'clock on Wednesday afternoon, I was still in the parlor trying to read the same page of *On Our Backs* that I'd turned to at eleven-thirty. My morning with Provincetown's finest had rattled me and I was still recovering when Loud Barb and her girlfriend came downstairs. The woman with them had a bad perm that left her frizzy hair free to wander all around her head. Loud Barb was jabbering in her ear like a happy idiot.

"We're going to rent some bicycles," the quiet woman said to me. Both she and Loud Barb wore black cycling shorts and long shirts that hung down over their wide asses. She said, "I keep thinking it's an awful shame about Joan." Her eyes were a little misty. "I never got a chance to ask her about her book."

"I had a racing bike once," Loud Barb was saying to the extra woman whose face was looking more and more familiar. "But I took it out to a cinder track once and just scraped the shit out of my knees and arms. No brakes on a racing bike. Don't you know, I sold it the next day."

"Do you know Helen Bowen?" the quiet woman asked me. "She's your neighbor since day before yesterday. Isn't that right?" The quiet woman squeezed Helen's arm in a girl's school kind of way.

"I sold it just like that," Loud Barb was repeating and Helen Bowen made a little bow with the side of her head, an acknowledgement that we'd met before though I couldn't say where. Her face had taken too much sun on its way to middle age and her eye makeup was pastel blue. It was a school of beauty that had lost out in recent years to realism. She had a complexion just like skim milk and watercolor eyes as cool and hard as bits of broken glass.

I made a point of studying the faces of middle-aged women for clues as to what was in store for me — now that middle age didn't seem so far away. In Sam and Naomi, I saw the regret Em kept promising I'd wear if I didn't straighten up and settle down with her. In Helen Bowen, I saw my full cheeks fallen into jowls and the lines in my forehead as deep as piping trenches. It was not a pleasant premonition. I thanked God that I would be spared her hair, an odd shade of blonde going fast to grey, but it was six of one and half a dozen of the other. My brown skin wouldn't line as fast, but I had to admit Helen Bowen had kept her body together and with my bad habits, you could bet I was going to seed.

I remembered then. The last time I'd seen Helen Bowen I'd been reading too. It was three days before, Sunday, after we'd come back from Herring Cove and Naomi was sleeping off her sunstroke. I'd settled down on the chair by the door with the Jeanette Winterson novel I'd brought for the beach but hadn't opened yet. I was making a note to myself on its title page to get a postcard for Em when Helen had invited herself in.

She'd shouted "Hello!" then walked through the entry hall towards the steps and stopped short when she saw me in the reading chair. "Oh, hello," she said again. "Do you work here?"

I told her I didn't, I was a guest.

"Is it nice?" She didn't wait for me to answer. "I'm hoping a room will open up." She dug around in her purse. It was deluxe size; she could have packed up her whole life and taken it with her. "Maybe you can tell me if Joan Di Maio is staying here?"

I said that she was.

Helen smiled into her open purse and lines spread out from the corners of her eyes like spider webs.

She asked, "Is Joan alone, do you know? I'd like to leave her a note. We met at a potluck in Boston two months ago and I told her I would look her up when I got to Provincetown. I'd like to leave her a note, but if she isn't alone, I'm afraid it could be awkward for her. You can imagine," Helen said.

I could imagine. But it was none of my business — who Joan was fucking, her litany of affairs, even if I didn't like it that the list seemed to be growing.

"Maybe I'll leave a note anyway," Helen said as if she had decided to give herself a present, and the lines around her eyes creased up again.

"I can show you where Joan's room is," I told

her, an attempt at Christian charity that didn't make me feel any better. "I'm Virginia. I hope you get a room." I didn't really.

Helen smiled again. "I'm Helen." She looked at my hand like she didn't know what to do with it when I put it out, but then she shook it like a power dyke. "This reminds me of my grandmother's house in Iowa," she said on the stairs. Her hand ran along the top of the bannister and she traced the outline of the knob at its end with her finger. "Just the carved wood bannister, that's all." She pointed at the window over the stairs and smiled. "And the lace curtains." The grey in her hair picked up the light like bits of silver.

She took a piece of paper and an expensive pen out of the purse and wrote a message. Then she folded it in fours and pushed it under the door of Joan's room.

"Thank you so much." Then Helen had turned and walked to the top of the stairs. She'd frowned at her shoes as if she were embarrassed to have talked so much to a stranger. "I can find my way out."

"Just like that," Loud Barb said, again engrossed in her own self-centered bawling, and her girlfriend asked for the second time whether or not I would join them on their ride.

"I was sorry to hear about Joan," I said to Helen.

"Oh," the quiet woman said. She asked Helen, "Did you know Joan too?"

"Not well." A fingernail-biting kind of look was sweating behind Helen's eyes. It was waiting to see if I would say we'd met before and where. When I didn't, her nervousness went away. She smiled at me as if we were co-conspirators and I smiled back, but I didn't like it.

"Anyway, I thought I was going to be a bike racer once," Loud Barb started up again, and all around I couldn't say I regretted that we were headed in opposite directions.

XVI

July 21

Tonight you die so I can live again.

XVII

At 7:00 on Monday morning I had been cinching up the drawstring of my sweatpants and stretching out as best I could, but my body didn't bend in the directions that it used to. In front of the mirror, it groaned and complained like old rusting machinery and my head hurt badly from last night's drinking. My body had betrayed me. It was a worrisome development because I knew the car girl didn't want me for my thoughtful soul.

In preparation I was jogging that morning as if a day of exercise would correct the lifetime of potato chips and beer before I had to take off my clothes. I was rebounding in the time-honored lesbian tradition. I told myself that there was something more to the car girl than sex so I didn't have to feel so cheap and easy, and that the exercise was just-in-case.

But really I knew better; it was the inevitable Sirens again. They were dancing me around to some Top 40 love song. Pretty soon, Em and I would be officially back on the rocks. But I listened to them anyway. Their voices were beautiful and I was weak.

Naomi was still snoring and mumbling in her sleep when I closed the door to our room. Outside, the hall was quiet and dark except for the light that came from under Joan's door. It lit my way to the stairs and at the end of the hall the loud woman snored. I stopped on the front porch to check my pockets for the house key before I closed the door behind me. Then I made for Franklin Street, already breathing hard.

The crowds were gone and I was alone in the street except for the garbage trucks stopped to pick up yesterday's remains. And every once in a while I caught a sticky sweet smell from the bags of trash leaned up against the fences around little shop-houses. Trash was piled in the alleyways. And down the alleys more of the same from the smaller shops set back behind the others. The garbage trucks and an occasional camper threaded their ways between the parked cars, and the men in heavy gloves rode hanging onto the sides of their trucks, shouting their good-mornings to the shopkeepers just sweeping off their stoops.

My watch read: 7:30 am, Tuesday. I was in front of Town Hall and I had meant to make it all the way to Race Point, but my ambitions were outstripped by my physique. I was sucking air at the end of the next block when I noticed Joan beside me. She was running the way that people do while they're waiting for the street light to change.

"Hi there," Joan said. Her nipples were hard against her shirt. "You know, I think we're the only healthy ones at Lavender House this week." I could hear myself wheezing but she didn't seem to care. "Anya and Sam refuse to exercise, but Anya keeps her figure anyway. If I didn't exercise, I'd fall apart." It was a lie. We both knew Joan's body was a brick. I figured she just ran to show it off. "Go figure Anya," Joan said. "I think that's what people mean by youth."

"Or genetics." I laughed and couldn't catch my breath. "I have terrible asthma, but my lover says she'll leave me if I get fat." I didn't want to tell Joan that my lover had already left me for other reasons. My body was gone to hell, but I still had my vanity and my pride.

"I don't care much for fat myself." Joan patted her washboard stomach. "But the salt air is good for asthma, I hear." She pushed our pace until I was having chest pains. "I run this way from seven-thirty to eight-thirty every morning." It was a kind of invitation. "You're not with your friend," she asked, meaning Naomi, and I grunted since I couldn't breathe deep enough to talk.

She said, "Oh, I didn't think so. She's really not your type; I can tell." Joan touched my arm like she owned it. "She's too self-absorbed. You need a woman who's interested in you."

"Thanks for letting me know," I said. "I'll call you next time I pick out a girlfriend."

"Please do," said Joan. And whatever "it" is, Joan had "it." She knew she had "it" and she didn't want you ever to forget that she was the kind of woman who could bend your mind. She smiled at me again with all her teeth as if I wouldn't present much of a challenge in that regard. And she ran me harder until I was bent at the waist, grabbing my calves to catch my breath again.

"I'm glad you're not with Naomi." Joan stopped and stood in front of me with her hands on her hips while I spat and panted at the sidewalk gutter. Her legs were apart and her thighs were in my face. I found their meeting and she smiled when she caught me at it. Her smile was pornographic and her legs made me remember Em's, as straight and tall as columns to a cool white temple, pale and hard as fascist art. On the inside of her thigh, Joan had a small tattoo; it was a tiny red rose with petals and thorns.

When I straightened up, Joan took my hand like I was lost. "That's not the way to get your wind." It sounded like a line — and it was. She said, "You have to cool down slowly," and she led me off the sidewalk back into the gravel lot where the new condominiums were going up. "The best thing is to walk for a while," Joan said. "Come on."

Construction on the site had stopped as if the developer had run out of money halfway through. The houses were cheap plywood frames waiting to be covered up with pre-weathered shingles, the window holes to be closed up with single-pane glass. They would sell for a lot when the next business cycle got real estate jumping again, but they were neglected now. We were alone and I was hyperventilating.

"Breathe deep." Joan put her hands on my cheeks and kissed me. Her mouth was hot against my own. "And slower," she said. She kissed me like she knew exactly what I wanted and she pressed me hard between her hips and the half-built frame that hid us from the street. I closed my eyes. She sighed and slid my jog bra up around my armpits. Her face was in my neck. Her hands were on my breasts and her breath was everywhere like steam. My arms were limp around her neck and she filled me with her fingers, worked them hard until I thought I might explode. My lips were blind. The world was dead; and all around me I could hear the rhythm of my breathing in her hands.

Later I asked if she was in love with Sam. It was a stupid question when I knew that Joan had sex the way that long-haul truckers stop for coffee. What I meant to ask was if she was in love with me. I needed to believe in love or else I'd have to deal with feeling cheap and tacky.

"I like Sam too." It was not the kind of answer I had hoped for. "She's great," Joan said.

When I asked about Anya, she kicked at the gravel. "Monogamy limits us."

"Right," I said and I asked her what Sam had to say about that. It was another stupid question.

"Everyone has to take power and responsibility in their relationships." Joan sounded like five years of weekly therapy, and another rationalization of why love affairs always seem to go to hell.

"And outting, is that taking power?" I said.

She frowned at me for a second and then smiled again when she'd figured out she could whip me in a political argument as well. "Sometimes," she said. "Every tool has its use. I keep a scrapbook of my columns. I'll show it to you sometime and you can decide for yourself." She looked over the top of her sunglasses and down her nose at the runner's watch on her wrist. "I have to keep up my training time," she said matter-of-factly, "but come by for a drink if you want." I watched her kick easily down the street. "Come have a drink sometime," she said again back over her shoulder, "you know where I live.

XVIII

At the breakfast table Loud Barb announced that she and her girlfriend were going whale watching. Loud Barb had both a camera and a pair of binoculars hung around her neck; she hadn't bothered taking them off to eat. " 'Be prepared' is what I always say." And her girlfriend nodded enthusiastically. They were dressed enough alike to be a vaudeville act.

Loud Barb gave me the high five as I was on the way to my seat. And Joan was saying she'd had another dream about the woman in the blue gown standing over her bed while the big white cats kicked sand around. In her dream, the cats ran away and the woman in blue reached down with both hands to throttle her until she woke up with the sheet wrapped around her neck.

Her hair was hanging wet in strings from running and the pieces twisted around her face like yellow snakes. I sat down beside her and Sam watched us as if I were stealing the silverware. And I thought Sam might have been Joan's nocturnal, Victorian lady in blue, all ready to choke the cheery sinfulness right out of her. Joan paused in her story conveniently to reach for second helpings as if the dream hadn't hurt her appetite. And I thought of my own fingers closed around Joan's white athletic neck.

"I could have sworn someone was strangling me." Joan held both hands up in front of the quiet woman's face and shook them savagely.

"Oh, my," the quiet woman said or words to that effect.

Loud Barb remarked that the bruise looked a lot like a hickey she'd had once and I felt obliged to kick Naomi under the table for laughing. I missed and my toes slammed into the table leg so hard they felt like fire.

"Sure looks like a hickey to me." Loud Barb crossed her arms. Her girlfriend blushed and nodded. "Well, I've seen my share of hickeys," Loud Barb said.

I rubbed my foot and the sides of Naomi's mouth crept up in a smirk that showed off her dimples before she settled on a more sympathetic face. "Was your tea a little hot, Gin? I'm awfully sorry," Naomi said. I doubted it.

"Are you okay?" The quiet woman dug an ice cube out of her water glass and held it out to me on a spoon. "Do you think it was a ghost, Joan?" she was saying. I chewed my ice and she beamed at me, all filled up with her own enormous helpfulness.

"Well, I don't know if she was a ghost," Joan said. "But maybe you and I could have a seance."

The quiet woman blushed again. "Gee, I thought they only had those in the movies."

"I have them all the time," Joan promised.

I didn't doubt it. I rubbed my toes underneath the table; I was sure the little one was broken. It showed on my face, I guess.

"Are you okay?" the quiet woman asked again.

"I'm fine," I said. "My tea was hot."

"Oh, burned your tongue." Loud Barb shook her head. "I hate it when that happens." She took a careful sip of her coffee and smiled from ear to ear when her tongue wasn't burnt. "I had an uncle from Rhode Island who saw a ghost once. Turned his hair snow-white afterwards. Well, that just about convinced me. Well, that, and that show on Public Television." Barb said, "There are all kinds of things we don't understand. And of course there's that Time-Life book series."

"It looks to me like that ghost bit her." Naomi creased up her forehead like she was worried that it was going around. "Pretty hard too," Naomi said.

She was grinning at me from behind her hand again.

Loud Barb clucked her tongue. "Never heard of a biting ghost."

"Looks like they're out there, though." Naomi pointed her fork across the table at Joan. "Will you look at that bite on her neck?"

Sam winced and Naomi said, "If that isn't proof, I don't know what is."

Loud Barb sent her tongue up against the roof of her mouth again rather thoughtfully. "There are things in this world we'll never understand." She put the side of her fork to her pancakes slowly, like she was considering great mysteries. Her cheeks belled out while she chewed and syrup came out of the sides of her mouth.

Sam said, "I could change your room if you like, Joan. I like my customers satisfied."

"That's something I'll be sure to keep in mind," said Naomi, but nobody laughed and I would have tried to kick her again but my foot was still burning from the last time.

"I'll move you downstairs, Joan," Sam said again. She made a face like something was hurting her, and Anya looked ill.

Joan promised she'd be fine and I guessed she hadn't spent the night alone.

"Did you get your message?" I was asking about the woman who'd left the note.

Sam looked like her lips were glued together and stretched out tight across her face. The look was calm but hysteria was leaking out at the corners.

Joan was so smooth she didn't even miss a beat.

"Sam," she said, "I met her at a potluck in Boston a couple months ago. She's here for a week and wants to get together. She's written a book and she'd like my opinion." Joan took Sam's hand, but it looked to me like a consolation prize.

"That's nice to run into someone you know away from home like that." Loud Barb slurped her coffee and grimaced. "Small world."

"Are you going to see her again?" Sam asked. It sounded to me like an ultimatum.

Joan was dancing. "She's just someone I met." She was sly and sheepish. "It's just that this woman has written this book and she wants me to read it, that's all."

"We'll talk about this later," Sam said, and I thought they probably would. Sam crossed her arms on her chest and I knew she and Joan were going to get into it long and hard. Loud Barb looked down at her plate rather sadly as if she would like some more pancakes. But Sam didn't offer. Barb covered her mouth and fought a burp.

Naomi said, "There was a fight down at Town Hall last night." It was a small kindness — for Sam or for Joan I couldn't tell which. But it cut the tension anyway and Naomi told the story about the town boy and the gay men of the night before like it was an epic. It was a good story really and Naomi liked to hear the sound of her own voice. "That's a funny thing isn't it," she said when she was done.

Sam shook her head and frowned. She said she knew the boy. He'd beat up on gay men before but usually he had a gang with him. Last summer, they'd jumped a man walking home from the beach on Route Six-A down by the lighthouse.

"Everybody knew who did it," Sam said, "but a lot of times tourists don't want to come back for the trial or they can't afford to come back, so these boys don't get prosecuted. Joan did her story on a thing in Dennisport last summer."

Joan said, "It was about how adolescents are threatened by gay and lesbian sexuality when they are just forming their own."

"There's a real psychology behind that kind of thing." Loud Barb had her finger in the air. "I say you have to address the psychology of the problem, just like racism or sexism." She looked at me significantly. "Well, isn't that right?" Loud Barb was demanding a minority opinion.

"I couldn't say," I said and she looked as if I'd let her down.

"Is there some kind of problem here with gay-bashing?" her girlfriend whispered.

"It's a kind of a perception problem," Loud Barb said. "Well, this is just public relations. Bad press can get you beat up." She stroked the back of her mouse-brown hair. "I know a little about public relations."

Naomi yawned obviously and Anya excused herself.

"No place is perfect," Sam said. "We have our share of problems, but we're better than a lot of places. The police want to prosecute at least because so many of our summer people are gay. And some of the guest house owners are trying to help out by putting people up if they have to come back to help prosecute bashers, so at least victims don't have to pay for a room on top of everything else. We just started it this year after Joan wrote her story; we'll see if it helps."

"Well, it's only now that the bars are even safe." Loud Barb stroked the top of her mouse-brown hair. "Of course, I'm not old enough to remember that, but from what I've heard, it used to be worse. You can't rush progress. Selling people on new ideas takes time." She gulped her coffee and coughed. "Down the wrong pipe." Barb coughed again and her friend patted her back gently.

"It's about time lesbians and gays did something to reclaim our own safety." Joan folded her arms across her chest.

"We're making progress though. You can't rush progress," Loud Barb said again.

"We're not making much progress," Joan said. "We could be doing more instead of blaming heterosexism on heterosexuals."

Naomi wiped her mouth. "Who do you suggest we blame this on?"

"That's exactly my point," Loud Barb said. "That's exactly what I was saying. This is a social problem." She was shaking her finger in Joan's face and Joan didn't like it. "There's nothing to blame but our social institutions."

"Oh please." Joan hit the tablecloth with the flat of her hand and the silverware jumped. "Why don't we blame it on ourselves and our self-hatred? Hate crimes happen because we're not visible enough. How many of you are out at your jobs?"

Her voice rose and fell like a storefront

preacher's. Call and response. There was no answer from among the ranks of the unsaved. It was just what she had intended and Joan went on calling: come to Jesus.

"By staying silent you condone their hatred of you. Every one of you, every time you fail to acknowledge that you are queer, you help some straight fascist put his boot on your neck. They are trying to take away all your rights." Joan opened her arms. "Virginia, you of all people should recognize this as struggle. And you ought to know, you and Anya, that struggle is sacrifice. This is *your* civil rights movement."

Her voice was mother-father promising that my Negro rights were well-secured and offering me the chance to fight for newer, whiter, more feminist causes. But I was tired of people saying what was good for them was good for me and I'd heard the pitch before.

"It's about you." Joan pointed her finger around the table. "You've all got to make waves. How can you expect elected officials to fight for you when you won't fight for yourselves?"

"I don't think all this has to be directed at me personally." Loud Barb was getting testy. "That's not very fair."

Naomi yawned again until tears came out of the sides of her eyes. Then she stood up from the table. "What I need is a smoke," she said.

"Of course this is personal." Joan turned up the volume like it was killing her to lose her audience. "You ought to know this is as personal as it gets. Straight people hate gays and lesbians because they don't think they know any. And they don't think they know us because we hide from them. Hate crimes will stop when we stop hiding."

Loud Barb said, "Some of us have to work for a living." Her face was red and her girlfriend was patting her hand.

"Some of us work for a better world." Joan hit the table again. "When public figures are closeted it hurts us all because we don't have them as role models and straight people don't know the celebrities they admire are gay or lesbian. *We* don't know that the people we admire are gay or lesbian. Really, you can extend that to everybody. Harvey Milk said everybody should come out so that straights could see the power and diversity of our community. When people harm us by malingering about their sexuality, we ought to pull them out of their closets by whatever means we can. I'm sick of turning the other cheek to protect the privilege of people who hurt us by the way they choose to live. The ends justify the means." Joan stretched her arms up over her head and left them there. "I pay my taxes and I say the Government ought to work for me."

"Well, that's all fine and good." Loud Barb wrinkled up her face like she was thinking very hard. "But I'd just like to know what finally happens with those people you're outing."

Joan had a sip of skim milk and smiled. "You know," she said, "I really couldn't tell you that."

XIX

That afternoon was overcast, and Naomi was sleeping. But I took a long walk anyway. I needed it. At the west end of Commercial Street, I turned onto the breakwater on a whim to see Long Point, the outward hook of Cape Cod where the land curls south and then east again. You could walk along Herring Cove beach with the curve of the land and you would come to it eventually, but that is a longer walk. It will take you well out of your way. From Commercial Street to the breakwater is shorter and that's the way I went.

The breakwater is a jagged pile of rocks thrown together in a line from the beach to the finger of the Cape, making a marsh from part of the bay. On the planes of the stones, there are broken shells and bits of crab the birds have picked over. There is straw pushed in between the rocks to fill the gaps. On the sides of the rocks the barnacles and seaweed have grown up high to where the tide has tried to reclaim them. At the bottom of the breakwater, low tide rushes out through the rocks across the flats like water over the shallows of a wide river heading out to sea.

Long Point was very far away, down the rocks and over the dunes covered with low brush and poison ivy. The rocks were sharp and uneven, the shadows of gulls were big across them when I walked carefully towards a place of American beginnings.

Long Point was the site of the first landing of the Mayflower in November of 1620. Had the Pilgrims been fishermen, no doubt they would have stayed at Cape Cod. But they were farmers and soldiers from a country that had become too small for them, they were boat people. What they coveted was land and Miles Standish marched his little sixteen-man army up the Cape as far as Wellfleet looking for Indians to mug for it. Finding none, they stole the corn that was standing in their fields and sailed off in December to the more famous second landing at Plymouth Rock some thirty miles away.

But Provincetown remains the signing place of the Mayflower Compact, the grandfather of the United States Constitution, and the top of the great, American domino chain. Settlement. Government. Commerce. Servitude. Slavery. Genocide. The white settlers spread themselves like lice across the North American continent on the backs and in the hair of others, exporting Christianity and smallpox. Good business.

In the 20th century a monument was built to this epic of success, a pale granite tower with square turrets. It sits on a hill to make it taller, surrounded by an undeveloped piece of fenced-off land over which it reigns. The Pilgrim Monument is filled with relics, the American history of Anglo-Saxons. It stands like a fortress against the ways of other peoples.

Standing on the breakwater you can see the Pilgrim Monument as the highest point in the low rise skyline; next is the Town Hall, then the

Heritage Museum, and the Universalist Church. Below them there are trees, the umbrellas of the Surf Club Restaurant, the beachfront porch of the Crown and Anchor, and the backs of the shops on Commercial Street. The monument watches over the town; it smiles down on the brisk pace of trade.

In its shadow there is a bus stop and sitting area, a semi-circle of flat grey granite where you can rest — briefly, though, as the stone seat is as hard as the Puritan ethic it commemorates. If you were to take this seat, you would have a view of the back of Town Hall, a deceptively large building which stretches from Bradford Street back to Commercial. Its windows are thin and tall, taking up most of its second story. There is a gravel parking lot in the back and a clock sits on its steeple. Above the bench in bas-relief metal is a depiction of the signing of the Mayflower Compact while women and children look on. The faces are thin and English; they are earnest and benign. One of the children, with his face turned upward towards his mother, wears a faint expectant smile as if he can read the future of a strong rich country full of weather-green statues and cracking monuments to dead white men. It is a country in which I can find no memorialized evidence of my own less auspicious landing some one hundred years after the mooring of the Mayflower at Provincetown. A legacy of exploitation and adversity, survival and resourcefulness. My absence in history and memorial is not surprising when people want to read stories with happy, unambiguous endings.

XX

The walk back to Lavender House was slow. The air was dead and it smelled like rain. But the first thing I heard when I got through the door was Sam screaming in the kitchen. It was a sound as ugly as being slapped awake from a good sleep and Sam's voice was pushed so high it cracked above the glasses she was pitching at the walls.

I heard: "Goddamn it, don't lie to me. You just can't help fucking around." I figured she could only be talking to Joan. She was.

"Goddamn it," Sam said. "I can take a lot but I can't take that, so just don't lie." More glass hit the floor, but Joan was cool as ice cream.

"I wouldn't lie to you, darling, I promise." Her voice sounded just like a foot massage — all ready to make you forget everything but the feel of her hands.

"You'd better not be lying to me, that's all," Sam told her. "I know who you are. So don't lie, all right? Because I just can't take it on top of everything else."

Joan laughed, but not like anything was funny. "Oh don't be crazy, darling. Don't be angry, baby," Joan said and I could tell she was finishing her sentences with her hands.

Sam told her, "You make me crazy all right. That's about all you've got going for you, and if you ever stop it you'll be out of here on your ass. You just remember that, okay?" She said, "Are you going to see her again?"

Joan didn't answer.

"Get out then," Sam said after a while. "Get your things." Her voice broke and she was crying. "You heard me. I can put a paying guest in your room tomorrow."

Joan's laugh was harsh and brittle. "You could put me out but you're not going to," she said, then she spoke as soft as melted butter. "You know, I've compromised my values for you, dear. If I didn't care what happened to you, I'd have turned that junior Republican hypocrite upstairs into an excellent installment of *Outtime*. But I've been protecting your business interests at the expense of my own convictions and you're going to let me stay here until I'm ready to go." Joan paused and I could imagine her lips slightly parted, promising opportunity. She said, "You know I'll do what I have to. But I'd love it, honey, if you'd just see things my way this once." And if I could have seen her face I knew it would be smiling in that this-hurts-me-more-than-it-does-you way.

Joan stopped again. "What's that?" she said and I nearly fell into the room when she opened the apartment door.

There was glass all over the kitchen and hanging in shards from the walls. Sam stood in the middle of the carnage with a dust pan holding the pieces of a big glass pitcher. I let my eyes run over Joan and down to the glass broken on the floor. Then I told them I wanted to use the phone.

"I have a long distance card," I said. "I hope this isn't a very bad time."

"Not at all." Joan smiled like sour milk. "I'm afraid I've dropped some dishes."

Sam ran her hand over her straight grey hair and sighed. "Why don't you let me meet you in the parlor. There's a woman to check in at four." She opened the door for me to go and held it like it was an order. "I'll show her to her room and then get back to you, if that's all right." She rubbed her palms against her apron. "There's a little bit of a mess to clean up here."

I said it looked like it and Sam closed the door. Anya was behind me, watching, when I turned to leave.

"I'm sorry you had to be exposed to that," Anya said.

I told her I was sorry too.

"It happens a lot." She tossed her hair. The sun had brought out the red in her skin. "Let's wait on the porch. Sam and Joan could be making up for a while." Anya rolled her eyes and led me out of the guest house. "I like it out here," she told me and I couldn't blame her.

It was getting hot again after a rain, but the street was wet. The cars went back and forth and their tires sprayed water at the curb.

"It's a nice place," I said. "It's peaceful."

Anya laughed. "Sometimes it is and sometimes it isn't." She asked me what I did in Chicago like she wanted to know.

"I tell stories," I told her. "I sell investment advice." And I asked her, "What do you do when you're not here?" She had told me before, but I had forgotten; she told me again and didn't seem to mind.

"I'm a senior this year at the University of Illinois. I'm going to Journalism school after college." She said it again as if she were making excuses for working the summer as a maid. "I want to get into Columbia. I've met some interesting people here. That's going to help me later on."

"Like Joan?" I said.

She shook her head. "Like the newlyweds in room four downstairs." She added, "Well, that's what I call them, anyway. It's that congresswoman from Maryland and her married lover that Joan was talking about to Sam in there." She was watching the slats in the fence around the house with her elbows on her pretty knees and she looked up quickly. "Joan would never do anything about her, though. Her voting record isn't bad enough. They come down here to cocoon and Sam brings them breakfast so they don't have to run into anyone who might know her."

Anya said that Joan recognized the congress-woman on the way to the beach and gave her a talking to about her politics. The congresswoman went crazy when she saw Joan coming out of Sam's apartment. "She and her girlfriend checked out this afternoon in a huff which is part of what the fight was about in there, even if Sam didn't say so. Business is business and she hates to lose a customer." Anya stretched on the bench and crossed her legs. They looked like three miles of milk chocolate. "Anyway, Joan wouldn't do anything about her I don't think, but Sam doesn't know that. Like I said, there are worse people. And her voting record's all right. Joan says she should come out anyway. But Joan says let the little fish go so you can catch the big ones."

"What do you say?" I thought it was a nice sentiment about the little fish and all, but Joan had been threatening pretty good in the kitchen.

Anya shrugged. "Joan says women shouldn't use economic power over each other. It's patriarchal. Anyway, with Barney Frank and Gerry Studds already out, she should take their example. They've both kept their seats."

"They're men," I said. "It makes a difference." I knew from experience. Out black lesbians didn't ever make partner regardless of their work. Sometimes closeted black lesbians didn't make partner either, even when they deserved it. But that was another more personal story. Married, white North Shore queens made partner though — all the time. "The rules are different for women," I said.

Anya tossed her hair some more and told me I sounded just like her mother.

"I feel about as old as your mother." I told her we old folks couldn't get behind the outting thing and she looked at me as if I were talking against trade unionism and apple pie. But on principle I don't turn in my own, even if I'm not crazy about their politics. It was a leftover thing my father taught me by example, telling us stories of the forties, and the people passing and exposed, those cream-colored, straight-haired products of half-forgotten rapes who were "known to have" a maternal grandmother in the woodpile. Middle-class black etiquette left them to their God, and their shame conjured demons because the world is hard and common ground is rare as faith and family. And you can't turn people into what you want them to be by wishing or bullying, though I can't say knowing better had completely stopped me from trying. But I imagined Joan might have turned in Homer Plessy for sitting in the good seats on a train from New Orleans to Covington, Louisiana and I didn't think Anya had bothered to listen when the old folks told their stories of the six million passing.

"Nobody deserves to feel unsafe," I said and I let my politics drop. I asked her instead how Sam had gotten tangled up with someone like Joan in the hopes I could talk myself out of it.

"Sam's getting over someone else, and Joan is Joan." Anya made a face and I couldn't tell if it was disgust or amusement. She said as far as she knew, Sam and her lover had bought Lavender House and rehabbed it from nothing. Maybe they were already on the rocks when they bought it. Anya said she only knew what Joan had told her about it. But the story was that the work held them together. When it was done they came apart.

"So now she's got Joan and maybe she's afraid she's going to be left again. I don't know," said Anya, "but you can't make someone stay around forever if she doesn't want to."

I nodded. It was a true enough sentence grammatically, but I wondered how much firsthand experience Anya had had with heartbreak. I hadn't been able to keep hold of Em myself; once broken we could not seem to fix whatever was wrong with our relationship. It was as if walking backward to undo what was done couldn't take you back to where you'd started. Even in apology, we'd wound up miles apart. Time changes things for sure, but the tough part is to let them go.

"Joan doesn't strike me as the nesting kind," I said.

Anya laughed. "If you want to know, Joan thinks of herself as a kind of a crusader for non-monogamy. 'If we ever hope to escape the patriarchy how can we adopt its standards for relationships.'" She was quoting Joan's cant like she knew it by heart. "The only thing is," Anya said, "I think Joan plans to single-handedly break up every exclusive relationship on the planet." Anya played with the ends of her hair while she talked and when she laughed again, the sound was harsh. "I won't knock her completely. Joan's taught me some things I won't ever forget."

I asked her if she meant about journalism.

Her face was stiff and her big brown eyes got hard. "No," Anya said. "I mean about power."

When I called her later, Em answered the phone on the second ring so I figured she must have been in the kitchen. She'd moved back in with her folks again. I knew how long it took for her to get to any phone in the house. When we'd first met, she would answer in the kitchen and then change phones for privacy. That afternoon she talked to me from the kitchen.

"Hi," I said. "I'm in Provincetown. Do you miss me?"

"What's to miss," said Em.

She'd hurt me and I'd hurt her. In my book, we were even, but not in hers. I could hear her extended family in the background speaking a language I didn't understand.

"I miss you," I said. "Is it hot there?"

"Sure," she said. "Is it hot where you are? How's Naomi," she asked like she didn't want to know.

"Naomi's fine." I told her I was fine too, and so was the weather. "I miss you," I said again.

"Hold on," said Em. There was a long pause and everything on the other end of the line sounded like Polish. Then Em told her mother she could hang up in the kitchen. "All right," Em said. "I couldn't hear a thing. I couldn't even hear myself think in there." We had a bad connection and I listened to the static in the line. "I miss you too," Em said like she had just remembered. "Have you met anyone?" she asked me.

"No," I said. To me, it was both true and false. To her it was just lying; she knew it.

"You can't help yourself." I could hear her sigh. "You don't even know what you want."

She was mostly right and that was what made me angry. What I wanted to hear was, "I love you whatever you do." I wanted her to say, "Everything will be all right with us." She didn't.

"Call me again when you know what you want," she said, but she meant I'd better want what she was wanting. She said, "Call me when you have your shit together."

I didn't hear the static anymore after that. The line was quiet and dead. I hung up too and went to find Naomi. She wasn't hard to find and we got some dinner.

The restaurant was off the Commercial Street strip and had a big painted bird on its sign. It was dark and quiet with rustic homemade kinds of furniture that looked like they came out of someone's summer cabin. I had a beer and a steak and Naomi had something more exotic and purportedly South American that she seemed to enjoy. The table was small, but the food was good. There were paintings packed on the walls of the restaurant Gertrude Stein-style. That was all right too and the waitress kept the bread coming. So, I didn't have any complaints. I told Naomi about the fight between Joan and Sam in the kitchen, and ordered dessert.

"That's a bite in the back." But Naomi seemed pleased. "Sam never did know how to pick 'em," she said and I didn't have enough stomach for malice to ask her what she meant by it.

After a while I paid the tab. We went out into the street and killed a couple hours walking up and down. Naomi said she owed me for dinner, but I didn't expect to see her half of the bill again.

XXI

Later that night, Anya was sitting on a stool beside Joan at the back bar of the Waterfront Dance Club. Joan wiggled her fingers at me, so I came over and took an empty place. Joan wasn't drunk yet but she was getting there and she was buying everybody's drinks so she wouldn't have to make the trip alone. I had a beer and Naomi had Stoli straight up; she was drinking in earnest herself since she'd discovered the drinks were free, and her neck was working on a swivel. Her straight brown bob was swinging back and forth around her ears like fringe. The bar was packed to the roof with girls.

"Your note leaver stood me up." Joan was sipping on her gin and playing with the glass. She looked past me towards her hopes of what was coming in the door. "She never showed."

I told her I was sorry to hear it.

Joan shook her head as if she couldn't imagine she'd been stood up and I had to admit it was pretty hard for me to fathom it unless the lady had caught wind of her personality; then it got easier to see. She waved for the bartender to come with another round and I admired the rock on her hand again.

"Well, I'm glad you're here." Joan's hand on my arm made me sick and wet. She squeezed my shoulder, hedging her bets and I waited for the bottom to fall out of my gut. "The least you could do is keep me company. That woman was supposed to meet me here by ten o'clock and Anya isn't feeling very friendly tonight. Are you, Anya?" Joan didn't wait for confirmation. She was watching Anya pout into her mineral water with the kind of pride in ownership my father used to reserve for big new American cars.

"I've got to go," Anya said like she meant it and

I followed her eyes across the bar until I came to Hillela in the line at the door. The line to pay the five-dollar cover was moving slow enough for Anya to be able to head Hillela off before she got inside. Anya got up fast and dug a couple dollars out of her jeans, laid them on top of the bar and turned to go. But Joan caught hold of her arm and wouldn't let her.

Joan's face was smiling, but her voice didn't match the rest of the picture. I'd expected she would be a nasty drunk and I wasn't much surprised. "Don't go. It's early, baby. And I get lonely," Joan said. "So, why don't you stick around until my date turns up." It wasn't much of a request, but she was holding Anya tight enough to make her knuckles red and it gave her a certain leverage.

"I really have to go." Anya looked down at her arm like she was thinking about gnawing it off. "Let me go, okay?" she said.

Joan smiled.

I was watching Hillela come across the room like the wrath of God, and so was Anya. So was everybody but Joan who was watching her own reflection in the mirror behind the bar, and she took her hand off Anya absently to fix her hair.

Hillela seemed to grow and spread as she pushed her way through the people on the dance floor, the way things that are far away get bigger as they close in on you. Her mouth was already telling Anya it was time to go when she got to the bar.

"Come on, Anya." Hillela was talking through her teeth.

Joan rattled the ice in her drink and smirked.

"Anya's tied up. But maybe she'll have time for you later. Well, your tough luck." She sounded like a playground bully and the blood rushed to Hillela's face like someone was squeezing it in through her neck.

"Come on, Anya," Hillela said again. "Come on, let's just get out of here." Her jaw was clenched and she was just about the color of cranberry sauce.

"Come on." Joan held her body like a threat. "Come on, Anya," she mimicked Hillela in a sing-song voice and then shook it off as if she were joking. "Hillela would do a lot better with women if she weren't so fat," Joan said to me like she was telling me a secret, but she whispered it loud enough that I didn't have to wonder if Hillela had heard and I was ashamed to be sitting next to her.

"Yeah, could be right." Hillela laughed like she knew how to take a joke. She said, "That may be right, but I've never had to coerce a woman to keep me company."

The color went out of Anya's face and Joan spoke slowly, choosing her words. "I wouldn't go much further than that, Hillela, if I were you," Joan said and her fist was clamped around her drink. She looked from Hillela to Anya, and her smile was unraveling at the edges. "I wouldn't push it because you're not the one who'll get the worst of it. I promise." Joan turned on her barstool and rolled the liquor around before she tipped up her glass. And I watched Hillela stand and shake for a long time before she walked away.

"I could kill you," Anya hissed in a way that might have been threatening if it had come from someone else. Anya left her drink on the bar and followed Hillela out of the Waterfront like she thought she'd had her revenge by leaving.

Joan watched her walk for a while and then shrugged again and ordered us another round. I watched Naomi drink, as I had lost the taste for mine. She tossed her Stoli back and licked the bottom of the glass to show off her neck for Joan when she was finished; and I was glad to notice the car girl by herself across the room. I left two bucks for my beer. Naomi had already squeezed in next to Joan at the bar before I could walk away.

The car girl wore red which suited her. I took it as a good omen that way that beginnings can always seem auspicious. The car girl, it turned out, was called Jo by her friends; it was short for Joanne. I thought of her, names aside, as the car girl, as if she had been born the minute she refilled our radiator. We didn't talk, so in actual practice I called her nothing at all.

That was fine with me and the car girl didn't seem to care. Names are for writing inside of anniversary cards and the car girl knew her hips were made to swim in. She took me to the dance floor and we swayed together until I felt like I was falling. She ran her lips along my neck inviting infidelities.

Later the car girl walked me out into the dark side-streets all full of people, a long walk on a warm night to the house where she was staying. The moon was out. She held my hand and the walk might have been romantic, but was not. It had instead a sad inevitability that mixes loss with anticipation. The loss was all the things I could imagine about the car girl before she would become, in intimacy, familiar; and all the ways I could dream she would make love to me before I knew. The anticipation was more commonplace. And the car girl said only that she had her own room by way of a definite proposal.

The car girl closed the door with my back and put her mouth on mine. She counted down my vertebrae and spread the cheeks of my ass beneath her palms. Her hands were cool and sure. I held my breath and her mouth was warm and soft, as pink and sticky as a child's. The wells of her ears that I found with my tongue were mild and warm like laundry soap and the place between her thighs dripped rain. It tasted harsh, the start of long regret, but the smell of her breath was sweet and sharp in the dirty sheet of her unmade bed. It was high risk activity in more ways than one and I didn't think about all of them until much later.

I lay back, instead, in the dark and she filled the empty space between my ears with moans. The car girl was all wordless sound and taste and smell. Her long tanned height was bent and sighing, was lips and breasts, was tangled in my legs and arms. We moved against each other slow and wet like hopeful hands around a magic lamp until she came, and went summarily to sleep.

And the car girl groaned. She rolled away from me with her beach-brown arms hooked underneath her pillow and her pale ass, lined with stretch marks, wide and shining like a second moon. I was waiting for her to help me lose my sadness. I was waiting for her to carry my losses away on her tongue and hide them deep in the cleft of her breasts. But the car girl only sputtered in her sleep. She twitched and jerked beside me and her presence filled the room like smoke until there was no air. She was like baking vanilla, so much better imagined than tasted, and I was careful not to wake her while I was making my escape.

We had folded our clothes on a chair by the bed. When we did it I couldn't remember. But I took the car girl's shirt from the pile and put it on. Like the room, it smelled of salt and stale tobacco. I left my own shirt in its place meaning this like an exchange of photographs between people who will not see each other again, the way you buy postcards in truck-stop restaurants passing through a state where you have never been before. Making memories of things you would otherwise let slip away. The details are saved in a postcard that works just like a time machine. It tells you who you used to be. It is remembrance and memento, and a trophy, something won at a loss. Years later, I imagined, when I wore the shirt I would remember the car girl, Joanne; Joanne, without it, would remember me.

I found my sandals on the sandy floor beside the bed and walked home without my underwear, whistling in the cool and friendly dark.

Lavender House was so quiet I could hear the floorboards creaking under the runner in the upstairs hall as I tried to mate my room key with the lock. I found the hole by means of an odd blue flash that came from behind me, like the light that comes with the opening and closing of a door. When I looked around, the light was gone.

I hugged myself and turned down the bed. Naomi had not been home and I fell asleep spread-eagle, tired and thankful to be sleeping alone.

I dreamed of Joan that night. We were running on the beach at Herring Cove buck-naked and she was singing: "The best things happen while you're dancing" like Danny Kaye from White Christmas. When I woke up I felt like a new girl; I thought I might run all the way to Race Point that morning, Wednesday. That was before I found out exercise could kill you.

XXII

Our room was empty when I finally got back to it after my adventures with the friendly guys at the Provincetown Police Station, but the bed had been made up and I found Naomi downstairs in Sam's apartment. Sam was sitting at her kitchen table, staring out the window over the sink as if somebody had wrung her out, the loud cotton pants she liked to wear looked slept in. Naomi was in a wooden chair beside her. I invited myself in and leaned against the countertop. The first thing that came to mind was that I would have liked to open Sam's refrigerator and eat what was in it, but politeness won out over hunger for a while.

"I'm sorry," was the second thing that came to mind and that's what I said. I asked Sam how she was getting along, but she didn't look good. Her eyes were bloodshot and her face was wet.

Sam blew her nose while Naomi asked in a motherly way what she could do as if she were actually ready to do what she could. The palm of her hand was going up and down on Sam's thigh like the tap of a metronome. The corners of her mouth turned up just a hair in an undertaker's smile. "I'm so sorry," Naomi said, and I wasn't sure I believed her.

I decided to open the refrigerator and help myself, since nobody seemed to be looking. I worked a beer out of the six-pack on the middle rack and closed the door.

Sam ran her hands through her hair and cried some more while we watched her. "By the time I was thirty I promised myself I would have a lover I liked, and a house that was mine, and a salary that matched my age. I'm going to be forty-one in November." What she'd thought would matter most at thirty was the last one, but she'd had the money, and it wasn't everything. "You know, Joan wasn't perfect, but I'd gotten used to her. This is really something." Sam shook her head.

I nursed my beer and did the same. But I've never been much good at grief and in this case it was all that I could do to sort my own laundry. I had wanted Joan, but I hadn't liked her; I'd liked the thrill she seemed to bring around with her and it embarrassed me that Sam's selfishness seemed to match my own.

"There are apples in there." Sam turned in her chair and pointed to the refrigerator door. "If you want some food to go with that beer."

I nodded, and ignored the dietary advice. "I'm sorry about Joan," I said again.

Sam laughed. It sounded nearly genuine. "I guess I ought to be comforting you." She dried her eyes. "You found her, right?"

I told her I was afraid the police thought I'd done more than that and it was going to be a chore to convince them otherwise. "Naomi says I'm in a jam," I told her.

"Well, look at it from their perspective." Naomi was rubbing Sam's leg in a way that looked pretty short of medicinal while she chattered brightly about my predicament. "You show up at the Police Station and say you've found a body. I'll tell you, people who find bodies are usually the ones who put them there. Any good lawyer or cop will tell you that. Murderers think it's cute to turn in the stiff so it throws suspicion off them."

"Thanks a lot Naomi." I sipped my beer and squashed the can. She always knew how to cheer me up.

"Well, no offense. I'm just telling you how it is." Naomi shrugged. "Would you rather I lied?"

"It'd be nice if you'd varnish the truth a little," I said. But I wanted to hear it. "It'd be nice to get some idea of how much trouble I've let myself in for."

Naomi crossed her legs like she was going to work the *New York Times* crossword. "Offhand, I'd say you're in for a fair amount. You found the body of someone you knew so I'd say you're it until the cops get somebody else. The police have got to figure they've got probability on their side with you and all they have to do is find a motive."

It wasn't a good answer. "Got any ideas of who really did it?" I said to Sam.

She blew her nose again into the ragged tissue and looked up at me blankly. "They questioned me as if they thought I did it too."

Sam said the police had come to Lavender House about nine that morning wanting to talk to anybody who might have known Joan Di Maio, starting with her. The Sheriff had sent his men to work upstairs in Joan's room and he'd called Sam into the kitchen, closing the door behind them for privacy.

He'd said, according to Sam, "Well, ma'am, this is a bad thing." The Sheriff had enumerated the ways it was bad, counting them out on his fingers as he sat facing backwards on the wooden chair where Naomi was sitting now. He'd looked at Sam across the table with a sad face and little shifty eyes. "It's bad for everybody," he'd gone on. "I want you to know I'm going to get this resolved just as fast as I can," and he'd rubbed his big hands together.

Sam said as an aside that she'd gotten unused to men. She didn't rent to them at the guest house. And so the size of the Sheriff's hands had amazed her. He'd wiped each palm on his pants legs and started his questions, writing her answers in a notebook he took from his back pocket and grunting to himself while he wrote. He'd asked, "Can you think of any reason someone'd want to kill this girl?"

Sam said she'd shaken her head and admitted

Joan wasn't what you would want in a dog. I thought it was a serious understatement, but I didn't think it meant that she was bad.

Joan wasn't faithful, but she hadn't made any secret of who she was or made many promises she couldn't keep besides the usual ones that are made in bedrooms all the time. The ones you can't remember making when they're repeated back to you in anger, implicit promises of exclusivity, that the touch of one woman in the whole universe of other women is somehow special. If you'd been misled with Joan, it was your own fault.

"I told the police that Joan pretty much saved her devotion for causes," Sam said, and she sighed. "That's probably what got her killed. Politics or women. Anyway, Harmon asked me if Joan was friendly with anyone in particular and we both knew what he meant. So, I told him she and I were friends."

"Friends or lovers?" I said.

"What are lovers?" said Sam, and I thought she was a lot smarter than me, but what else was new?

She said Sheriff Harmon hadn't liked her answer either. He'd cleared his throat and tried again. "Did she have a special romantic interest, I mean," he'd said.

And Sam'd told him she didn't know of anyone that Joan considered special. Not being sure of who else might have been in the queue, Sam said she hadn't been about to volunteer herself as a particular love of Joan's. I couldn't really fault her and I found myself wondering where I had ranked.

Without trying, or rather it seemed in trying to save herself the trouble of a painful police investigation into her sex life, Sam had put her finger on the thing about Joan that was truly profane. It was that Joan left you with the feeling she could have been with anyone else and it would have been all right with her. Not, of course, when you were with her — that was her special magic — but after she'd gone. Joan left you with nagging doubts. Like sleight of hand, when you know there has got to be a trick somewhere, but you can't seem to find it. I thought: that was Joan all over and the trick was everything there was. It was everything and nothing. It was two white doves pulled out of thin air.

"Wasn't there anyone at all?" Sheriff Harmon had put his pencil down on the table and laid his arms across his gut as if he were an immovable object it would be tough to get past.

Sam told him she really couldn't say who all Joan slept with and it pleased her, she said to me now, to realize it was the honest truth. She had stared the Sheriff down until he bent his head over his notebook and blew out his breath. "He asked me what Joan had been doing in Provincetown and I told him she was writing her book on hate crimes. That was all he wanted to know," Sam said. "He told me he was sorry again to have bothered me, that was all he needed for today. He said he had some pretty good leads and the police were optimistic they would be catching whoever did this to her." Sam began to sputter again. She bit her lip and then spilled her guts.

Sam was just over forty and her lover had left

last fall after the season with one of the sixty thousand summer people who come to P-town every year, a New York management consultant. In the same way some people come to Provincetown to drop out of the mainstream for the summer, Sam's lover decided it was time to drop back in; and she walked out after Labor Day. She left Sam the bed and breakfast they ran together or that is to say she left her the mortgage. She took the dog, which broke Sam's heart.

Joan had stood as a stop-gap measure against her loneliness which was most severe in the crowds of summer people that filled up the streets and spilled out every day onto MacMillian Wharf by the boatloads. Their lovemaking, Sam said, had had the tentative feel of a summer rental.

Naomi made a comforting sound in her throat. She was kneading Sam's pants leg like dough. It was just her thing. This kind of sad seduction. Naomi covered Sam's hand with her own and I watched her fingers play with Sam's ring. I wondered where I'd seen the ring before.

"You know I've always cared for you." Naomi wet her lips like she was threading the eye of a slim opportunity. She looked down at the table like a bashful movie lover.

I tossed my empty beer can in the trash bin I'd found underneath the sink. "I think I'll go out to the porch," I said. But nobody seemed to care and I helped myself to another beer for the road.

I was still drinking on the bench by the door when Anya came up the front stairs. She carried a backpack over one shoulder like a purse and was wearing the same clothes she'd had on in the bar the night before.

"I think you'd better sit down," I said. "Did you know someone's killed Joan?"

Anya sat and said she'd already heard. But she started to cry anyway as if she had determined a display of grief was in order. I watched her sniffle into the neck of her oversized T-shirt. "I'm all right," she told me, although I hadn't asked, and she dabbed her mascara with a piece of tissue she took out of her front jeans pocket.

I looked at painted boards in the floor of the porch and told her I was sorry. I was saying that a lot lately and I worried pretty soon I would be so numb I wouldn't mean it anymore.

"Thank you." Anya took my hand and squeezed it. She managed to look both coy and suffering all at once. She said the police had asked her to tell them everything she knew about Joan and she had done what she could to help.

"It's really a shame," I said.

Anya dabbed some more at her eyes and put her hands across her lap. "Yes it is. Joan was a wonderful woman." She squashed the dirty tissue in her fist. "She had some wonderful ideas. I told the police she was an activist."

On the road beyond the fence, cars were passing back and forth. "It's got to be worse for you," I said, "since you were so close to her." I asked her if that was all she could think of to tell the police.

Anya nodded. "Well, they wanted to know if Joan was seeing anybody. Of course, I thought they would have known about Joan and Sam from talking to

Sam but they didn't. I told them that," Anya said, "and that Joan was living here for free. They can draw their own conclusions, I guess."

I wondered what Anya's conclusions were. When I asked her, she tossed her head like a horse. "I thought Joan was using Sam. But I didn't share that with the police. I think there are other women Joan would rather have been seeing." Anya wrinkled up her nose. "But I really couldn't say, you know."

I didn't. What I did know was a cop sat in a squad car across the street and I wondered if Anya had told the police about her own dealings with Joan. I'd seen them fighting on the beach the afternoon before Joan died.

That afternoon Herring Cove had been almost deserted. I had been looking forward to a chance meeting with the car girl but there was no sign of her or anybody else when I'd laid my bag down on the sand. I was sorry I hadn't had any lunch, but the hike to the concession stand wasn't something I was up to after humping it all the way out to Long Point. I spread out my towel instead, well above the high-tide collection of debris and promptly fell asleep.

I dreamed of the beach in Delaware when I was a child. The water had been like this, churning hard under an angry spitting sky. I'd been taken by the undertow and swept slowly down the beach without realizing it, sucked into deeper and deeper water until the lifeguard girl pulled me out and threw me on the sand. She was bending over me and I could hear my mother screaming. All I could see was blue water the color of a clear hot day falling over my head. In my dream, the lady in blue and a big blonde lifeguard took me up in their arms.

When I woke up, it had started to drizzle. The clouds hung low on the sand like car exhaust condensing in the cold and the waves frothed white at their tips, the water pitched and heaved itself at the horizon. It was pouring miserably by the time I had gathered up my things and I held the beach towel above my head, walking out towards the parking lot through the dunes, hoping that the bus to town was still running.

There was no bus in sight. The rain was falling in sheets on the parking lot and Joan Di Maio was standing beside a rusted out Chevy, the only car in the lot. She was screaming at Anya. I wanted a ride, but not badly enough to put myself in the middle of it.

"Why don't you just get in the fucking car," Joan was shouting.

Anya was shaking her head. Her heavy hair was matted on her head in clumps and she didn't look so beautiful in the rain. Water ran down her face and she wiped it away with the side of her hand like she didn't mind being wet.

Joan stamped her boot. "Oh, come on. It's fucking pouring, Anya." The wind whipped her hair around in strings that smacked her in the cheek with every gust that came up, and blew her shirt flat against her chest.

"It's too damn cold for this." Joan raked her hand through her hair and sighed and shrugged. She kicked the ground and sighed again. She threw her hands up and said, "Look, I'm not going to tell anyone. All right? I promised I wouldn't tell and I won't. I'm not going to write any letters either. You just need to see things my way. Can't you see things

114

my way?" Joan got into the car and waited. She rolled down the window and the rain ran down the inside of her car door and onto the back of the seat. "I love you," Joan said. She said it like the words were so familiar she didn't have to think about them any more. She said it because she thought it was something women liked to hear and I was frosted because Joan could tell she hadn't had to say it to me.

"Sure, I love you too," Anya said. It was obligatory, like a greeting on the street when somebody else speaks first. Anya shook the water out of her hair like a wet dog. Then she opened the car door and got into the passenger's side. She let Joan lean across the car seat and kiss her. They stayed like that for a long time with the engine running and the windows steamed.

I came down from the top of the dunes along the path after the car had pulled away and I didn't mind the rain anymore. I was feeling cheap enough to need washing off and after a while I caught the bus near the end of the parking lot.

The ride back to Lavender House on the rehabilitated school bus was slow as crawling, but all of the walking had made me tired and hearing Anya tell Joan she loved her had made me sad. It felt good to lean my back up against the window with my feet on the seat.

I hadn't seen the fake green leather of a school bus pew since my graduation from high school some ten years ago. As a kid I was bussed because I lived more than a mile away from the only school in town. The bus stopped at the corner and took me into the country so far out of my way that I might have made better time by walking. But the long bus ride on a winter morning seemed then, as now, a small luxury. It was a ride filled with the faces of neighbor kids who I knew so well that I could tell them by their voices in the dark carrying over the vacant lots and used-to-be corn fields that were the perimeters of my girlhood. It had been no preparation for the larger perimeters of a world filled with enemies and strangers.

Now the bus wound along down Route Six-A towards the guest houses on Bradford Street. Its engine grumbling, the bus passed the postcard dunes grown over with low bushes and high eel grass instead of the flat open fields of my home town, rolled along a marsh near the point, past the lighthouse at the end of a long stone jetty and then on into town. The ride called back the lurches and bumps from past commutes and the sullen loneliness of the child I was twenty years ago, an anomaly on the seaside roads to the all-white beaches of the Delaware shore. And though I hadn't thought of it in years I wanted to see my father's summer house again, if only to feel there was someplace where I belonged.

"So what did you tell the police about you and Joan," I said to Anya, and her eyes turned into little slits.

She let herself back into the guest house through the screen door before she answered me. "I have to get to work," she said, but she might as well have said, "Fuck off." Anya turned on her heel and left me watching her back cross the foyer. I made a promise to myself we would talk some more as soon as she'd finished up the toilets.

* * * * *

When Naomi came out to the porch, she had that look of successful seduction. Her face was flushed, she was out of breath and vaguely happier.

"What are you looking at?" Naomi blushed some more for no good reason and took a cigarette from the pack in her pocket. She rolled her lighter around in her hands for a while and looked at the painted boards under her feet.

"How's tricks," I said. "Or more to the point, how's Sam?" She gave me a face that was blank and inscrutable — the thing it lacked was an innocence which for her was not at all unusual.

I said, "Doesn't this affect you?" What I meant was isn't it scary that one day you could be running along and somebody who doesn't like you could get a gun and blow you out of existence. I was talking about the randomness of life and I wanted us to have a focus group about it, but Naomi wasn't much interested in philosophy.

She smiled. "Virginia, I want you to think about who got killed." Naomi tucked the cigarette in the corner of her mouth and lit it with finality. "This was not exactly Mother Teresa we're talking about and besides, the police can't tie people up in a vacation resort — whoever did it is probably already gone."

That wasn't my point.

"Of course the cops still have you to think about. I'd stay on my good side," Naomi said. She squinted up her eyes and grinned. "Where's your date this morning, anyway?" She meant Joanne, the car girl.

"It didn't work out." It was both an over- and an

117

understatement. The evening had been a horrific disappointment as a day in my life, but in the grand scheme of things Joanne was just another one of my missteps on the way to old age, one more wasted evening in four years of a dying relationship, just another night of fucking around. Susan Coogan was the top of the slippery slope and everything after that just got easier.

Naomi hung her arm around my shoulder and squeezed my collar bone so I would know she liked me particularly. "What you need is a trip to the beach." She winked.

I asked her what the cops were going to do about me and she shrugged as if the thought no longer interested her. "Nothing. What can they do? You'll be gone in a week — they can't keep you here unless you give them a good reason. They'll leave the file open and after a while they'll forget about it."

"I don't like the idea of my name in some police file forever," I said. "It's like being a criminal."

"Not a criminal — a suspect." Naomi sat down on the steps and blew her cigarette smoke at the sky. "Let's go to the beach," she said again. "Come on." The clouds were burning off and it was getting hot.

I said, "You know, if we were trying to figure out who did this, I wouldn't be a suspect anymore. Isn't that right?"

Naomi looked doubtful. "Could be." She rolled her tongue around her cheek. "But I'd leave it alone if I were you. You're not really a suspect. The police are just interested, that's all."

Somehow it didn't make me feel too safe. "Who do you think did it?"

"That's hard," Naomi said. "I mean, take a number." She blew out her smoke in a pale thin cloud. "That *Outtime* column couldn't have made Joan any friends. You know, Sam's mystery guests in the room downstairs were a conservative congresswoman, married, and her very young female companion."

I told her I'd heard about the congresswoman from Anya so I figured it couldn't be much of a secret. But I asked anyway, "What if Joan was blackmailing her or threatening to out her?" But I was just exercising my vocal cords mostly. I got up and walked around the porch to give my legs a workout too.

"No dice." Naomi shook her head. "They checked out the day before Joan got killed. She flew back to Washington yesterday afternoon."

"What about Sam?" I said. "She didn't like it that Joan was carrying on."

Naomi shook her head again, and harder. "Not a chance." But I wondered where Sam had been when I'd come home from the car girl's place the night before. "Can we go to the beach already?" Naomi said.

I said, "I wonder what those women from Vermont had to say to the police."

XXIII

Loud Barb and her girlfriend had the room at the end of our hall by the stairs, the biggest room in the guest house. I thought their bed looked wider too. Barb was saying they'd made reservations nine months in advance because she was so particular about her accommodations, among other things. Her girlfriend nodded and looked around their room as pleased as if she'd invented it herself.

Loud Barb said, "Girls, you're just in time. We're just about ready to go to the beach." She was wearing neon green surf shoes. An inflatable rubber raft was propped up beside the bed. On the wall hung a framed print of two cherub-faced little girls in pastel dresses on a divan with a litter of black puppies. Somehow I was not surprised.

"What I like best about this place is that the choice of furniture is so consistent." Naomi leaned against the door frame and grinned. "It makes me just want to run right out and have my apartment redone."

"Do you think so?" The lines in Barb's forehead buckled up. "I like to think our room is different from all the others."

I told her I thought Naomi meant the rooms were uniform in their individuality.

Naomi said, "That's exactly what I mean."

"She's kidding you," I said.

"Oh, well. That's what I thought." Loud Barb looked pleased again. "Do you like my water socks? I say for the beach, they're the only way to go."

"I'll bet," said Naomi.

The quiet woman nodded. "Barb says: 'the right shoe for the right sport.'"

"Only way to go," said Loud Barb.

I asked her what sport in particular her shoes were for and she looked back at me like there was air between her ears. "You got me there." She slapped me hard on the back and then she slapped Naomi too. "You got me there. I guess you wouldn't call beach-going a sport, would you? Would you call beach-going a sport, honey?" she asked her girlfriend who shook her head. "You got me there," Loud Barb said again. "Anyway, we were on our way to the beach when the police showed up this morning and we haven't got there yet. Otherwise we'd be gone by now. That Sheriff talked to us for nearly an hour."

"That's a while," I said. "What did you have to say for an hour?" I sat on the edge of the bed near the raft. Their window looked out on the backyard and a quiet side street. Out there was Sam's vegetable garden and a squad car parked behind the picket fence.

"Not much." Loud Barb waved her hand. "Come on and make yourself at home." She beat on the top of the bed and waved her hand again at Naomi to sit. Naomi didn't and Barb went on, "I told the police I didn't know Joan except from breakfast. And Jane told him that business about the ghost."

The quiet woman was saying she had judged the

cop to be a very nice man. He'd said he was from Springfield and the quiet woman's dead father who was also a nice man had come from there.

Loud Barb shook her head. "Damn unpleasant woman, that Joan. Of course, I'm sorry she's dead. No one deserves to be dead." She took hold of her girlfriend's hand. "But I think she wanted Jane."

The quiet woman said she doubted that but she looked as though the thought pleased her anyway.

"No. No. No." Loud Barb slipped her hand around the quiet one's waist and squeezed. "I'm positive, honey. Oh, that woman wanted you all right." Loud Barb said she could always tell. "No hard feelings, though." She added, "I'm awful sorry she's dead. That's what I told the police."

"Thanks a lot," I said.

"Oh, not at all." Loud Barb got up and stuck the inflatable raft in her armpit. "Don't forget your water socks," she said to her girlfriend. To me she said, "Are you sure you won't take a ride out to Herring Cove? Saves gas."

"We really have to be going," I said. I was hoping we wouldn't run into Loud Barb at the beach.

XXIV

At Herring Cove, Naomi leaned her head back in the lounge chair to sun her neck while the heavy girl poured oil on her shoulders. I watched the cigarette smoke roll out between Naomi's teeth. The car girl sat Indian style on the blanket beside me. She was just the same, but the thrill was gone and I'd not meant to run into her again.

"Why'd you leave last night?" The car girl's pride was hurt and she lowered her voice so that her friends wouldn't hear.

I was pushing the sand back and forth with my feet. "I don't know. I like my own bed. It's familiar." I buried one foot in the sand with the other. "I was drunk," I said finally. It seemed like the best excuse.

"Did you take my shirt?" the car girl asked. The hair on her legs had turned blonde in the sun.

I looked at the legs and thought of my trophy. She was watching me with her face all puckered up from thinking hard and I told her, "I don't know anything about your shirt."

The car girl kept her face scrunched up and asked me what I'd worn home when I left.

"I wore my bra and my jacket." I thought I was turning into a pretty good liar. "I couldn't find my shirt."

"I have it, actually." The car girl shrugged and looked at her hands in her lap. "Actually, it's too small for me."

The curly-headed girl turned on her side in the chair. She held her head up with her elbow and examined her arms. They were red with freckles and shiny from the oil. Her arms looked like they hurt and her nose was blistering badly. "I wish I was black," the curly-headed girl announced. She smiled at me. "You're so lucky," she said.

Naomi snorted. She rolled over on her back and the heavy girl looked at her with lust.

"Really," the curly-headed girl observed. "If I was black, I could get really dark. Look at me." She held out her arms deep with freckles. "If I was black, I could get a beautiful color."

"Sure," I said, "but then you'd have other problems. I promise."

"If it's not one thing it's another," the curly-headed girl agreed.

Naomi shook her head in disgust. She broke her cigarette off in the sand and dug in her bag to get another one.

"You want some more oil on your back?" the heavy girl asked her.

"I must have lost my shirt on the beach." The car girl pulled me down beside her on the blanket. Her body felt heavy on top of mine and I thought it was one of her best qualities. "So, what do you really want?" the car girl asked. There was an offer in her question, but the mystery was gone. "You really want your shirt back, baby?" the car girl asked.

"Yeah." I told her I really wanted the shirt. "Can you bring it tomorrow?" I reached for the beer I'd stuck in the sand and watched her sideways to make sure she seemed genuinely disappointed. She did.

I was smiling pleasantly to myself until I saw the steel blue of a policeman's uniform behind the dunes. It ruined my mood. I remembered the police cars in the yard and I was starting to wonder if the cops were following me. I slapped Naomi on the leg. But when she looked the uniform was gone.

"Keep your shirt on, Virginia," Naomi said. "Relax." She told me I'd probably seen a park ranger. But none of the topless dykes on the beach had called out the usual warnings and I wasn't so sure Naomi was right.

XXV

"I bought these earrings for Louise in Wymon's Stuff," Naomi said. I had waited outside because I couldn't bear to watch. For all of Naomi's faults, she used to have the kind of pragmatism that I admired — that survival instinct. Used to be I knew if it were me and Naomi in a one-man raft and a big blue ocean, I didn't ever have to worry about her losing sleep over the obvious decision. Now, it looked like the lesbian breakup demons were carrying Naomi away. Those voices in your head that reasoned if you liked your ex-lover well enough to sleep with her, how come you can't meet for coffee once a week and buy each other presents for the rest of your life after she leaves.

There is good news and bad news in lesbianism. The good news is you don't have to worry about getting pregnant. You don't have to worry (much) about getting AIDS. The bad news is oppression by the patriarchy, and having to go to potlucks and places where people use words like "patriarchy" and "herstory." The worst news is that you don't have the dissonance-reducing options of heterosexual women who can reasonably chose to view their lovers as members of another species, proof that the organs of simpatico are often housed below the waist.

Naomi and Louise might patch it up enough to exchange presents, but I knew, when it was over, that Em and I would not be friends. Emily is like that. Morality for her is black and white. It comes from that Catholic school training, heaven or hell. Second chances are like purgatory, a place I'm told no longer exists.

"So what's with you and Sam now," I asked Naomi.

She smiled like she was keeping secrets and listed out the recent improvements: "She's not mad anymore. I think we can communicate. It's nice." It seemed to me an understatement now that she and Sam were cozy as clams. I was going to ask what she'd done to manage it, but then I saw Hillela Hill.

She was rumbling through the street like a city bus and the crowd was parting in front of her to give her room. Cars stopped. She was walking fast with her black clothes for the night's show in a plastic dry-cleaning bag and she kept turning over her wrist to check her watch like she had somewhere to be. I put a hand on her arm and hung on, but Hillela kept moving.

"Hey," I said. "Remember me from the beach?" She looked down at my hand on her arm, and then up at my face with a move-it-or-lose-it kind of expression I thought I ought to take pretty seriously, but I gave her a smile that showed all my teeth and hoped that that would hold her. "Listen, I passed out those flyers for you. I got rid of them all." It was a lie. But it stopped her long enough for me to introduce her to Naomi and ask if the show was going well.

Hillela stared at me like I was selling something she didn't want. She was going to cut me off mid-pitch and her face wrinkled up getting ready for the big no.

"Did Anya catch up with you last night?" I said.

"What?" Hillela's eyes were so small it was hard to tell what color they were. They were rimmed in laugh lines, but she wasn't laughing. "What about Anya?" She squinted hard like she couldn't place my face, but she'd decided now she wanted to remember who I was.

"Last night, you left the waterfront and Anya ran after you. I saw you," I said. "And I wondered if it had a happy ending." It was my best-friend voice, but she knew we weren't best friends.

Naomi rolled her eyes indiscreetly and I didn't appreciate it.

"Right." Hillela folded her cleaning in half. The

plastic crinkled under her hands. "Right." She stared hard at me again for a second and began to walk off.

I went along beside her, Naomi hanging onto my arm, but the street was filled with people and she kept getting further away. People were closing ranks behind her like something out of *The Ten Commandments* and the space between us was filling up with bodies until all I could see was the back of her head like she had waded into deep water. "Hey Hillela," I shouted. "Did you know that Joan Di Maio's dead?"

Hillela stopped and turned around to look at me.

"Joan's dead, did you know?" I said again while Naomi held her hands over her eyes and grimaced. She was watching through the spaces between her fingers like our conversation was a scene from an Alfred Hitchcock film.

Hillela looked like she knew about Joan. She looked like she was trying to place my face. "Who are you?" Her hands were rolling the plastic around her cleaning with a life of their own.

I said, "I know you fought with Joan the night before she died." I thought it was the kind of bold declarative sentence that drove out confessions, but I was wrong. She just stared at me some more. So, I said, "I just want to know what you said to the police, all right? I want to know if you told them the truth because I want them to find out who killed her."

Hillela shut her mouth and opened it again. "I have to go. I'm late for my day job." She pressed her thin lips tight together and stared at me as if I were crazy. I was, kind of.

"Don't you care about this," I said. In the street some Jersey-looking guy was whispering into his girlfriend's neck. He stopped to look at me, and Naomi was pretending we were unaffiliated.

"I'm late for work." Hillela wound her cleaning into a ball around the hanger and held it under her arm. "I'm really late." She walked off first slowly and then more quickly. I watched her shake her head until she'd disappeared back into the crowd.

Naomi tapped me hard on the shoulder. "What exactly do you think you're doing here?" she said. She had a hand on each hip.

I said, "I want to find out who killed Joan. Look, maybe she was a friend," I said. I was trying on the word for size. But it didn't fit. A lot of what I felt about Joan didn't fit. She was a nasty collection of appetites: sex, ambition, power, all those things we're not supposed to want but everybody does.

I told Naomi, "You have to ask questions to find out things, right? And it doesn't seem to me like we have a whole lot of time left. You already said the killer is probably going to get away."

Naomi dropped her hands and sighed. "Look, Virginia, you're not very good at this." She put her arm around my shoulder. "Buy me a beer and I'll give you some free advice."

XXVI

The bar was dark and cool and empty. I liked
that there was no one to share it with and I closed
my eyes.

"I'll tell you what you ought to do." Naomi waved
the bartender over. "Relax," she said. "I'll tell you
something about the police."

According to Naomi, the policeman's rule was
simplicity: the direct solution was the best.
Convoluted motives and purposes were for Perry
Mason and Nero Wolf. For the regular guy it was
straightforward thinking that would get him where
he wanted to go. "The cops think maybe you did it
because it's an easy guess," Naomi said. "And if they
can't figure out why you'd want to do it, they'll look
to somebody else, probably Sam. You didn't sleep
with Joan did you?" Naomi asked. "I didn't want to
get into it in front of Sam."

I told Naomi she gave me a pain.

"Don't get testy," Naomi said. "Everybody else
slept with her and you've never been noted for your
judgment, Ginny. But that's one good thing. If you
didn't sleep with her, you probably didn't kill her."

"Of course I didn't kill her," I said. "So the
question now is who did?"

"Look at it from the cop's point of view," Naomi
said. "Let's say you didn't do it."

"I didn't do it," I said.

"Right. You didn't do it," Naomi went on. "So the

cops have got a lesbian corpse that everybody figures for a player; everybody knows Joan slept around. She's shot up close. The conventional wisdom says it would take somebody Joan knew pretty well to get within five feet of her at five o'clock in the morning. Chances are whoever shot her probably knew her real well, if you follow me."

I followed her but it didn't make me feel any better. What I was feeling could have passed for jealousy if Joan had been alive. Since she was dead, I didn't have a name for what I was feeling in the pit of my stomach.

"So, the cops have got to figure this for a crime of passion," Naomi said. "There's only one thing about this that bothers me — the note."

"What note?" For a woman who had found the body I was starting to feel a little out of it. Naomi and the police had this pretty much sewed up from the way she was talking and I was still trying to get over the shock.

"There was a note stuck in the pocket of her shorts. It said, *'You deserve this.'*" Naomi told me it had been written on one of the pads from Lavender House. "The cops are checking the signatures on the canceled checks for the rooms to see if they can find a match with the note, but I think it's a long shot. They can't hold anybody here if they want to leave. There've been some hassles over Miranda when the cops tried to tie people up at a crime scene without arresting them, and with every day that passes the killer could have left P-town."

Naomi scratched her head. I watched her scalp jump up and down. "I'm telling you," she said, "the police were hurting themselves trying to have a look at the pads in our room to see if they could pick up any impression of what had been written on them. If that stupid deputy asked me if I had a piece of paper one more time, I was going to scream. But they can't search the rooms without a warrant which may be hard to get for anyplace other than Joan's room without probable cause since she didn't die at Lavender House. Until they get enough for a warrant, all they can do is come around and hassle the patrons a little and Sam's not going to like that much." Naomi winked. "Bad for business."

I asked her how she was so sure the police didn't have enough to search Lavender House already.

"I know because they haven't done it yet. Believe me, you'll know it when they have enough." Naomi took a drink of her beer. "They're looking for a love interest or a grudge. Whoever shot her didn't care about money. Her wallet was still in the back pocket of her shorts. The cops found thirty-seven dollars, three gas company credit cards and a dog-eared Lavender House business card with Sam's personal number, handwritten on the back. Sam's handwriting didn't match the note they found in her pocket, but they're going to send it to Boston for confirmation anyway."

"Where did you find all this out?" It amazed me that I had turned in a body and spent three hours that morning at the police station, but nobody had told me anything. They'd just asked me questions and then looked like they didn't believe the answers.

"Professional courtesy." Naomi shrugged. "I asked."

"Who do you think did it," I said

Naomi looked into her beer. "If you want my opinion I don't think we'll ever know. Sixty thousand-some-odd people come in and out of this little town all summer and Joan Di Maio made a profession of making people mad. Relax," Naomi said. "Take a number; whoever did this to Joan has probably come and gone. So, let's have our vacation, go home and forget it."

But I'd seen it and I couldn't forget. "What about Sam?" Naomi had told me before — the last time I decided to play Philip Marlowe — that people get killed by people they know. I reminded her of it. "What about Hillela? Jealousy is the oldest motive there is and you saw them get into it at the Waterfront last night as well as I did. Or did it ever occur to you that maybe Sam got fed up and did her in?"

Naomi lit a cigarette and coughed. "I think I had better tell you a story," she said, and I could tell it was going to be a long one. "When I was in college I thought I was straight but with other interests if you know what I mean. Do you know what I mean?" Naomi looked sideways at me without moving her head. The look was shy and sweet and I wouldn't have believed it of her if I hadn't seen it for myself. "In my freshman year, I met a woman who seduced me. She was older than me and I got drunk and I slept with her on a dare one night." Naomi was blushing under her tan. "Everybody's got a story like this."

I said it seemed like they did. "When I was in college, I slept with my roommate." That lover seemed very long ago. I said, "I think everybody has a coming-out story."

"So, shut up," said Naomi. "I'm telling you mine, I'm sharing." She blew her smoke at the ceiling. "Anyway, I found out I liked girls and we lived together then, this woman and I, after that. She'd wanted me all along, you understand. Women liked me when I was young and guileless — at least she did."

I told Naomi she'd never been guileless.

"Well, maybe not." She studied her beer. "But you never forget your first girlfriend. Am I right?" Naomi said, "Do you know what I mean?"

"Sure," I said. I thought she was right and I wondered where my first lover had gotten to.

"I was hot when I was young." Naomi raised her beer and laughed. "You can't imagine."

"You're still hot," I told her. It's what friends are for.

"Do you think so, really?" Her reflection was tan and arrogant behind the bar. She smiled at it. "You know, I think you're right. I've still got it," she said. "Well, when I was young I had my offers. I slept around on this girl and of course I got caught because I was so young and stupid."

"Guileless," I said.

"That's right." Naomi tapped her finger on the bar. "I didn't know how to get away with it then. Let me tell you, it takes the wisdom of age." She smoked while she thought about it and then crushed her cigarette out in the paper ashtray. I drank my beer and I waited for the story to go on.

"So, my girlfriend caught me," Naomi said, "and she threw my shit out of a third-story window." She raised her shoulders and dropped them again. "Well, she caught me in our bed. You can imagine."

I told her I couldn't and it made her mad.

"Everybody cheats," Naomi said and I thought she was probably right, but the cynicism of it still brought me down.

"Everybody cheats," Naomi said, "that's the thing. If it's not at one thing, it's at another. That's what this girl was too hard-headed to understand and I was too stupid to get away with, that's all." Naomi rubbed her forehead. "But it wasn't pretty. She moved out after that and I finished school. I've always regretted it — the cheating part, I mean. That was a misstep." Naomi's Marlboro jiggled in the corner of her mouth and she cupped her hand around the flame of her lighter. "But what I'm telling you is Sam Flynn was my first girlfriend," Naomi said.

It made so much sense it made me laugh. I told Naomi I thought I'd heard it all now, and I asked her if she thought any of it had a point.

Naomi rolled her cigarette on the side of the ashtray and took it up again. "The point is if Sam were going to kill anybody, she would have killed me. You know she really loved me. So, Sam and Joan fought about sex, who doesn't? Sam's a big girl and she knew what she was getting into with Joan. The point is, it still doesn't make a bit of sense. You have to know about people." Naomi took a handful of peanuts from the bar. "You have to have a nose for these things. Now, I know people," Naomi said. "I know Sam. And anyway, why would Sam leave a note when everybody knew what Joan was about? Why leave it for Joan's benefit? Before she got shot, Joan knew she was fucking around. After she got shot, she was dead. Like I said, it doesn't fit the facts."

I looked at myself in the mirror behind the bar. "So what? So it doesn't make sense to kill somebody out of jealousy? It's not rational but people do it every day." I picked up my beer. "Tell me it doesn't happen all the time. And I think they were fighting about Anya. She was standing in the doorway listening when I turned around. What about that? That kind of thing ought to count for something."

Naomi told me I was watching too much TV.

But what I know is: it's the little things that become intolerable; the larger indignities we bear. "What about Hillela?" I told Naomi about the fight at the beach and my talk with Anya on the porch, but she didn't seem too impressed. I said, "You're still in love with Sam, aren't you?" I thought it put things in perspective.

"You never forget your first," said Naomi as if I'd asked her opinion on dietary fiber. She looked down at her nails and chewed the side of her thumb. "But seriously, Virginia, I think you ought to let this lay. There's no reason to believe whoever killed Joan is someone you know. Sure, people get killed by people they know, but Joan knew a lot of people you don't. If you keep pulling these stunts like the one with Hillela, you're just going to piss people off and you won't accomplish anything."

It sounded like she was making me a promise of failure. I argued, "What about the kid we saw fighting at Town Hall that night? Sam said he's beat up lots of people. Sam said he was sort of crazy. You'd have to be crazy to shoot somebody in the head like that. Maybe it was a hate crime. Joan wrote a story on hate crimes in Dennisport, last year."

"Too easy." Naomi shook her head and smiled at me as if I were stupid. "The cops would never have missed that angle. Besides, how do you explain the note on guest house paper? The guest house was open all day and anybody could have picked up a pad, but it was definitely women-only space."

I thought my beer was getting warm. "Maybe it's a coverup."

"Forget it," Naomi said. "The cops look one hundred percent better if they catch a killer fast rather than dragging it out. Better for business. I'll bet you a beer to a bagel the kid has an alibi."

There was a film of dead foam on the inside of my glass. I slugged my beer and washed it away. I said, "Maybe it was revenge for one of Joan's *Outtime* articles."

"Maybe." Naomi yawned.

"Joan kept a scrapbook of her columns." I wondered aloud if the police knew it was around. "You know, I could tell the cops about the scrapbook. I could tell them about the fights with Sam and Hillela and Anya," I said. "I mean I saw them firsthand. And at least they'd have all the information."

"What makes you think Sam and Hillela and Anya lied to the cops? I think you ought to lay off Sam and everybody else, is what I think." Naomi was getting mad again. "Lay off for your own good because the more interested you seem in this thing the more suspicious the police are going to think it is. You're just going to buy yourself trouble with this in the end."

I thought she was probably right.

"You're never going to know. Whoever killed Joan is probably halfway to California." Naomi sighed. "I wish I were halfway to California."

"Do you think the police know about the ghost?" I said.

"Now that's a thought." Naomi ground out the butt of her cigarette.

"All right," I said. "Forget about the ghost."

"Don't you listen, stupid? Barb's girlfriend already bent Harmon's ear about it."

"Don't call me stupid, all right?" I said.

Naomi rolled her eyes again. "Then do me a favor and forget all about it because it's just not your forte. Remember what happened the last time you thought you were Nancy Drew?"

I was trying to forget, but the memory still felt like a bleeding ulcer. It was just like Naomi to pour salt on the wound.

She put ten dollars on the bar. So I figured she was sorry. "Look," she said. "I know you don't run across dead bodies you know every day. It's upsetting, sure. But don't worry." Naomi squeezed my shoulder hard. "I'm going to think about this."

XXVII

"Well, I don't think that's fair at all." Loud Barb looked like she might be having a brain aneurism. I had heard her shouting the minute I walked in the door. "The police were right there in our room when we came in. I think my constitutional rights have been violated and I know a little about the law," said Barb.

"I let them into my apartment and Anya's room," Sam said. "Then they wanted to see the guest rooms. What could I do?" She opened up her arms in appeal, but it was getting her nowhere. "I was with them all the time. They didn't disturb anything," she said.

"It's a good thing too," said Barb. "I know my rights." Her girlfriend stroked her wispy hair. "I know something about the law," she said again. "This business is invasion of privacy."

They were all in the parlor, Loud Barb and her girlfriend, Sam and Helen, when we came in.

"We've had a little excitement this afternoon," Sam told Naomi. The police had a call that said they ought to search the Lavender House if they want to find out who killed Joan. Sheriff Harmon asked if they could look around and I told him they were welcome. But Barb here came home and took exception."

"Well when we came in the police were in our room," Barb said. "For chrissake, I don't see why they should be welcome in our guest room without some kind of official papers when we haven't done anything wrong. Our guest room is exactly where they aren't welcome." She raised her butt off the couch and then set it down again. "I didn't see any papers, did you Jane?"

The quiet woman shook her head.

Loud Barb said, "That's exactly right and when I got done with those boys they beat a trail out the door. I'm telling you. I won't have some men going through my personal effects."

Her girlfriend patted Loud Barb's knee. "Oh you were very fierce; you were wonderful, dear," the quiet woman said. "It made me afraid, just watching you."

"I have half a mind to check out of here tonight," said Barb.

"I wouldn't do that if I were you," Naomi told her. "I don't think I'd change my plans at all unless I wanted to look suspicious to the police."

"Suspicious." Loud Barb's voice had gotten even louder than usual. "I don't think I've had a suspicious day in my life. This is Nineteen Eighty-Four, that's just what this is, this is positively Orwellian, that's what it is." She looked pleased with her choice of words.

"We just don't want the police going through our things." The quiet woman blushed and I thought of dildos and vibrators. The cops going through Barb's sex toys almost cheered me up. But Naomi was frowning hard and Helen Bowen was looking sicker by the minute.

"No offense, Sam," Helen said, "but I'm glad I'm only registered until Friday morning." She smiled like she was having her teeth pulled. "A day and a half more of this is about all I can take until I'll need another vacation."

"Well, we must get your address," the quiet woman said. "Now don't forget."

Helen said she wouldn't and Loud Barb grunted, "Well, this can't be very good for business."

Upstairs in our room things looked pretty much like we'd left them. Naomi's clothes were everywhere so even if somebody had ransacked the place you'd never have known it.

I lay down on the bed to take a nap while Naomi had her third shower of the day, but I couldn't sleep. Every time I closed my eyes, I saw Joan on the ground at the construction site, shot in the face. It wasn't pretty. So I got up and made a tour of the room, straightening. It's a trait I inherited from my mother.

When I was twelve, my mother went back to work and we got a cleaning lady, an older southern woman who'd come north in the great black steel migration. Flossie came once a week when we were younger and twice a month after I'd left for college. She ate all the candy in the dish on the coffee table and she drank up my father's gin on the sly. She vacuumed and dusted and did the laundry, but Adeline and I had to clean our own rooms. We resented that and having to clean up before and after Flossie as my mother could not bear for anyone to think she couldn't keep her own house.

Since Em had left, I'd craved for order in my

surroundings since I couldn't seem to have it in my life, and I picked up after Naomi that afternoon for the comfort of familiar activity the way some people turn to prayer. With Naomi around, I knew that order wasn't something that was going to last, but I hung up her pants in the closet and parked her shoes under the bed the way I used to do for Em because it took my mind off Joan. I put the room keys in the water glass on the dressing table and opened the little drawer underneath to put the stationery away. That was when I found the gun.

I shouted and Naomi came out of the bathroom. She wore a towel on her head and a blank expression and I held the drawer open for her to have a look. "Fuck," she said. "We have got some problems now." She rubbed her forehead hard. "You didn't touch this did you?" With two fingers she picked up the gun by its trigger guard and held it up to her face. It was silver and square. Naomi announced it was a .22 automatic. "It's not loaded," she said, "which is good and bad." Then she put the gun on the dressing table and sat back on the bed.

It was probably the same kind of gun that killed Joan. Naomi said the police had found spent shells at the construction site and maybe they could use them to tell if this was really the gun that killed her. "Twenty-two caliber bullets deform when they hit things, even pretty soft things," Naomi said, "like muscle and bone. So it's hard to match them to a specific weapon. But you can match a gun to a murder weapon from the shells sometimes. When the gun is fired, the bullet casing in an automatic gets kicked out the side. A specific weapon leaves marks on the casing just like the grooves in the muzzle leave marks on a bullet. If this is the gun that killed Joan the police can check its ownership by looking up the registration."

I was glad to see Naomi knew her stuff. It made me feel like my tax dollars were really at work, doing something other than financing transfer payments. Not that I'd begrudge anybody money to keep themselves fed, but it made me feel like I was getting a little something out of government services too.

I said, "So the police can tell whether this is the gun that killed Joan from the casings they have." It sounded like good news to me. "Why can't we just tell them we found it?"

Naomi put her arm around my shoulder and her face so close to mine I could see the pores in her olive skin. "Let's think about this for a minute, Virginia. You found Joan's body and now you've found the gun that maybe shot her in your room."

I was starting to see the problem.

"What we ought to do," Naomi said, "is take this thing out to the beach tonight and throw the son-of-a-bitch into the ocean. Someone else will find it and turn it in. The police will have another piece of evidence maybe, and you and I won't be involved. Since we don't know who this gun is registered to and it doesn't belong to me or you, right?" Naomi waited for me to shake my head. "I really don't think it's constructive to distract law enforcement professionals with ourselves as suspects. It doesn't help Joan and it doesn't help us. I say we ditch this thing and go on about our business. All right?" That's when I told her again that I thought the police were following me.

This time she looked like she was taking me seriously, but it wasn't making her very happy. "Are you sure?" Naomi asked. "How many times do you think you've seen them?" She took the towel off her hair and dropped it on the floor by the bed. Her hair had clumped and she teased it into shape with her fingers.

I told her I'd seen the police at least four times since this morning and she frowned. "Bad answer. Are you absolutely sure, Virginia?"

I told her I'd seen them outside the house twice, at the crosswalk by MacMillian Wharf and at the beach. Naomi ran her hands through her hair and groaned. "Well that's a horse of a different color. You've got to ditch this thing inside the house. If the cops see you pitch a gun into the ocean, we're really fucked. Let me think about this." After a while she said, "There's an umbrella stand in the hall. You can stick it in there while I keep watch. Five seconds and our problem's solved." Naomi looked pleased with herself. It was a shame I couldn't feel the same way.

I said, "How come I've got to get rid of the gun and you get to watch?"

"I thought up the plan." Naomi picked up her towel again and rubbed it over her hair. "I can't be expected to do everything. Besides, you found it."

"We could draw straws," I said. "It's fairer."

Naomi put her hands on her hips. She was short but tough. "I'm not touching that fucking thing again. Better for you to go to jail than me."

It was my own thinking, exactly, the law of the jungle. But the deed got done.

* * * * *

We ate at the Stagedoor Cafe that night. It had a comedy club above it and Kate Clinton was playing, but I'd seen her show just a few months before. So we sat by the window and watched the free show in the street instead. Naomi had the fried calamari and I had a hamburger and some beer. We both got drunk and Naomi ran through the litany of suspects without my encouragement: Anya, Hillela, Helen, the congresswoman and a space Naomi left open called TBA. Naomi was taking the thing with the gun as a personal affront. Frankly, so was I.

"Why would the killer put the gun in our room?" I said.

"They knew you found the body." Naomi's eyes were so angry they were nothing but yellow iris. "The keys to the rooms are on a hook in the kitchen of Sam's apartment. It wouldn't take an international jewel thief to get them, but I'd make a bigger bet on somebody who already had easy access to the room keys, like your buddy Anya. And I think we ought to go talk to Hillela tonight after her show." Naomi was deadly sober all of a sudden.

I said, "I thought you told me to leave well enough alone."

Naomi said, "I think I've had a change of heart."

XXVIII

Hillela Hill was playing the back room of a place
on Commercial Street called Jocelyn's, a dark place
with no windows, a few chairs and a pool table
whose felt was shiny. But before Hillela's show the
women were three deep at the bar and the room
was close with the heat of people's bodies.

After the show, Jocelyn's was quiet. The
out-of-towners had gone off to the dance bar. The
regulars, with the place to themselves again, had
their elbows on the bar and their hands in the nut
bowls. They were a used-up threadbare collection of
women. And the bartender was a dyed blonde in a
low-cut blouse. The skin across her chest looked
striped from sun wrinkles. But she knew what her
regulars drank and she didn't have any illusions
that she was pretty. She asked where we were from
as if she might have cared.

Naomi told her Chicago and ordered herself a
vodka. She said, "My friend will have whatever
you've got on tap."

"Long way," the bartender said, "Chicago. Just
the same we get more midwesterners than you'd
think." She set up the drinks.

Naomi paid and pushed a single across the wood
at her. I raised my glass and watched the bartender
look Naomi over. "First time in P-town," the
bartender said.

I told her it was, but she wasn't talking to me. She leaned over the bar with Naomi's change and nodded. She ran her tongue across her lips and said, "Is it your first time here," as if she hadn't asked the question yet.

"First time in a while anyway," Naomi said.

"Glad to have you back." The bartender wiped the counter and made small talk until a regular called her away. When she came back over, she had another drink in her hand. "On the house." Making a gracious gesture with her arms, she set the vodka on the bar in front of Naomi. "Complimentary to returnees. I'll even bring one for your girlfriend."

"I'm not her girlfriend." I laughed. "But it's getting to be a common mistake."

The bartender spread her arms again. "In that case, I'll bring you two."

"Why don't you do me a favor instead," I said, and asked, "Would you happen to know if Hillela Hill is going to be here tonight? I'm looking for her."

"You and everybody else, honey." She waved her hand like she was shooing flies. She drew another beer and told me again it was on the house. "Star-struck women are always looking for Hillela after the show. That's how she got hooked up with that girlie who stays over at Sam's."

"Anya?" I said.

"Yeah, her." The bartender took the tea towel off her shoulder and dried some glasses in the little sink behind the bar while she talked. "Anya works over at Lavender House for Sam Flynn. Now that's a pretty girl. She and Hillela have had a thing all summer, on and off. Summer gossip." The bartender turned around to Naomi. "You looking for Hillela too?"

"I'm just lending my moral support," Naomi said.

"Good for you." The bartender cracked her towel like a whip against the bar and put it back on her shoulder. "Women get a little too caught up in celebrity if you ask me. They lose sight of what's important. Nobody wants a regular girl anymore. That can make it lonely." She pushed her hair off her face and leaned across the bar at Naomi as if she was going to tell a secret. "Now, you don't look like you'd ever be lonely," the bartender said.

"You'd be surprised." Naomi looked down at her drink and then at her fingernails. "Sometimes I'm a pretty sad girl."

The bartender wiped a glass. "You don't look sad to me." She whispered, "You know that Hillela has a lot more charm on stage than off."

"That so?" I said.

"Don't get me wrong." The bartender put her glass away, picked up another and rubbed it with her towel. "Hillela's a friend of mine. She's a funny woman."

I asked her how she meant it.

"Oh, I don't know." She laughed and it made deep lines on the sides of her mouth that weren't dimples. "But, if you're looking for Hillela she's here with her manager most every night after the show. All you have to do is wait." She looked at Naomi. "Wait long enough and I get off at two. The name is Gwen. G-W-E-N."

Naomi rolled her eyes at me.

"Can I get some service here?" A short-haired

woman was tapping her change on the bar. "I don't have all night — anymore." The regular looked like five miles of bad road.

The bartender whispered: "She likes for me to keep them coming."

"So, was Hillela in here on Tuesday night for instance," I asked her.

"Are you sleeping over there Gweny?" the short hair was saying, "cause I can take my patronage somewhere else just as easy as here."

"I'm coming. Keep your shirt on, honey. There goes my tip." The bartender winked at Naomi and made a dash across the bar. "See you later. It's been a treat, ladies," she said.

I asked her again, calling out the question if Hillela had been in the night before.

"I can't talk now." The bartender, Gwen, waved her hand at me. "I work for a living. But here comes Hillela and you can ask her yourself."

Hillela sauntered in and sat down heavily at the opposite end of the bar. She looked like her feet hurt. She waved to the bartender to bring her whatever she usually had. It came on the rocks in a highball glass. Her manager sat down beside her and the bartender brought her a club soda.

"Come on," I said to Naomi and slid my glass down the bar to where Hillela was drinking. She looked up when I put out my hand. "Virginia Kelly." I took hold of Naomi by the arm. "And Naomi Wolf."

"Were you at the show?" the manager asked.

"That too," said I. "Good show."

"We met this afternoon." Hillela looked as if it was something she'd have liked to forget.

I shook the manager's hand. "But we haven't

149

been formally introduced." I made myself comfortable on the stool beside Hillela, but she didn't look happy about it. "Why don't you let me buy you a drink and we can have a talk," I said. "So, what do you say?"

Hillela turned her back to me on the barstool in a way I had to take for disinterest. I can't say that it hurt my feelings much.

"Why don't we dance," Naomi said to the manager who batted her eyes. Naomi put a quarter in the jukebox for a slow song and they went away.

"Come on. What will you have?" I was holding my money in the air.

Hillela brought my hand back down against the top of the bar, banging my watch on the wood. "I think I can manage," she said. "Put your money away."

"All right," I said. "Relax."

"Cut the shit." Hillela put her elbow on the bar and wiggled her fingers for the bartender's attention. She got it and ordered another gin and tonic.

I said, "Tonic will put the weight on you."

Hillela pretended she hadn't heard it. She thumped the bar in front of me with her open palm. "My friend here will have whatever she's been drinking."

"Beer," I said.

"Beer," said Hillela. Her face was balled up like a fist and her lips had started working, getting ready for the punch. It came when Gwen the bartender had gone, in a long creative string of words that used the hard k sound and I asked her if that was what she'd said to the police.

She said, "What exactly do you want?"

"I'd just like to know where you were last night."
I was still smiling but Hillela wasn't. She hunched
over the rest of her drink and aimed her eyes at the
bottles behind the bar as if I were an eyesore.

"What are you," Hillela said, "an admirer?"

"I thought you only had eyes for Anya," I said,
but she didn't think it was very funny.

"Let's make this short," Hillela said. The words
came out as if she was pushing them through the
spaces in her teeth. "I was here last night after my
show, all night. Ask Gwen if you want." She pointed
to the bartender who came over then with the
drinks. She put my beer in front of me on a fresh
cocktail napkin and smiled at Hillela for a tip. She
was the only one smiling.

"You make friends fast." The bartender looked
sadly at Naomi slow-dancing with Hillela's manager.
I thought: hope springs eternal.

The bartender said, "It's too bad everybody isn't
that friendly."

"She wants to know where I was last night,
Gwen." Hillela picked up her drink and put it down
again.

"Well, like I told you she's here every night after
the show." Gwen took the towel off her shoulder and
wiped the top of the bar. "She was on that same
stool right there from about twelve o'clock last night
until last call around two in the morning and her
girlfriend was with her."

Hillela nodded. "I told you so," she said. "Anya
and me are off and on, but we're usually on again
by bedtime. She was with me until the police
showed up this morning. Were you thinking maybe I

151

got up early and killed Joan Di Maio before breakfast?" Hillela's teeth were white and pointed. "I'm sorry to have to let you down."

"I'm sorry too," I said, "but thanks for the drink." I wasn't so sure she'd let me down. There are a lot of hours between two o'clock and five o'clock, but I didn't tell Hillela that. I stood up and pushed my beer bottle towards the back of the bar.

"Oh, finish your beer," Hillela said. She wasn't angry anymore and she leaned her shoulder at me in a friendly way. "You're not so bad," she said, "and I'm starting to like you a little." She showed me what "a little" looked like with her thumb and index finger. "Listen, I knew what Joan was about and I knew she slept with Anya, all right? I won't say I liked it."

I told her it hadn't looked like it.

"I won't say I liked it." Hillela ran her hand over her hair. "But I couldn't stop it; I don't own Anya. I just love her and I didn't want her fucked over. I didn't want Joan trying to take her away. After I figured out Joan couldn't do that, I didn't care what they did together." She laid the cocktail straw on the side of her napkin and took a sip of her drink. "I hope this isn't a newsflash for you, but it ain't a perfect world."

I told her I'd noticed.

Hillela raised a shoulder at me and then let it drop. "So, why don't you take your drink and your friend over there someplace else now and give me some peace." She waved for her manager who was leaning over the jukebox writing out her number for Naomi on a cocktail napkin. Then she looked back at me like it was time for me to go. And I moved further down the bar by myself to nurse what was left of my free beer.

Naomi was wearing her lady-killer grin when she came around. Even bad news couldn't wipe it off.

"Where are you when I need you, prosecutor?" I said. "Hillela claims she was with Anya all night, here and at her place until the police came around this morning." My beer was warm and flat. I picked it up and saw the film over top of it, then set it back on the wood. "So, maybe they really did do it together. But Anya doesn't have any reason and Hillela doesn't really strike me as a murderer."

"Nobody strikes you as a murderer." Naomi put her elbows on the bar. "What is it I keep telling you? You have to know people, Ginny." She sipped her drink and grinned some more. "Besides, it sure looked like she wanted to kill you."

I didn't appreciate her humor. "Yeah," I said, "but she ended up buying me drinks and telling me about the world. I don't think she could stay mad long enough to stake out the Lavender House until Joan got ready to run this morning." I figured Hillela would have had to sit out there all night to catch her.

Joan had told me when I'd seen her the day before that she jogged on a schedule of seven-thirty to eight-thirty. But she was already long dead when I found her at a little after seven. I didn't know what that meant. "This beats me," I said.

The bartender was cracking her towel on a glass to impress a redhead with a crew cut.

"What was that all about?" the manager was saying to Hillela. The manager pointed her thumb down the bar at Naomi and me and Hillela downed her drink.

"Nothing," she said. "Don't I pay you to keep the groupies away from me?"

I left another dollar on the bar and pushed the door to Jocelyn's open with my shoulder. "I still want to talk to Anya. Maybe they killed her together."

Naomi sat down on the curb by the bar. "I doubt it. It's too complicated and Anya doesn't have any reason." She rubbed her eyes with her fists. "Did I tell you, I heard from Sam about that town boy? He was in jail again for fighting and drunkenness the night Joan was killed. Apparently his family wasn't willing to bail him out twice in one week. They thought it would do him good to spend the night in jail."

"I guess it did," I said. "Which just leaves the other guests and Anya — or Sam." I raised my eyebrows at Naomi and she didn't like it. "So where do we go from here?"

"Let's go dancing," Naomi said.

XXIX

It was after midnight when we got to the Waterfront. The car girl had found herself a cover-girl blonde with spiked hair and a short skirt. The heavy girl and the one with curly hair were nowhere in sight. The car girl bent close to the lipstick blonde. She wouldn't meet my eyes across the bar and I figured my shirt was as good as gone. I chalked it up to experience.

"You do look good in clothes," the car girl was saying to the blonde.

Naomi was talking politics with a Smith girl who looked way underage. "Mystery novels can never be truly feminist," the Smith girl said, "because they must either assume that the state of the world is good and our system of justice is benign or that things are so screwed up there is nothing the individual can do about it." The Smith girl ordered another gin and tonic and Naomi handed the bartender a twenty.

"Do you see what I'm getting at?" The Smith girl wrinkled up her forehead.

Naomi smiled. "Oh yes indeed."

I was watching the car girl across the room. She turned to her date. "You wait here, baby." The car girl picked up my shirt from the seat of the chair beside her, kissed the blonde goodbye at the V of her open neck blouse and sauntered over to the bar.

"I brought your shirt," the car girl said. It was

clean and she had folded it, but she'd left her beer back with the blonde who was pouting now with her cover-girl lips stuck out and red.

"Thanks." I liked the shirt. "Where are your friends?"

"We're leaving tomorrow," the car girl said, and explained that her friends were packing. "You smoke?" The car girl tapped a cigarette on the edge of the bar. She offered it and I shook my head.

"Good for you." The car girl lit her cigarette, then dragged on it and held the smoke. "I'm trying to quit," she said. "So, you want to meet my friend?"

She pointed so that the blonde could see she was telling me who she was. The blonde perked up. She gave us her profile.

"She's pretty," I said and the car girl remarked that the blonde was a quality woman.

The car girl cracked her gum. "Not that you aren't quality too." But we both knew my behavior had been cheap. We both regretted it. "If you're ever in the City, babe, look me up. I'm in the book." This was something the car girl said a lot. It fell off her tongue and I was relieved to hear it. She said, "You never told me what you do in Chicago."

"It's complicated." I knew the car girl wouldn't appreciate my attitude, but I didn't care. We were through, she and I; and we both of us knew it. I said, "People don't usually understand what I do."

"Try me," the car girl said. "If you can explain it, I'll bet I can understand."

"I write about what stocks to buy." I began what I intended to be a long scientific explanation.

The car girl nodded, but she was watching her

blonde. "That's nice," she said. "So if you're ever in the City .. "

I smiled at her as if I nursed regrets. "So, this is goodbye," I said.

"So long." The car girl kissed me open-mouthed. She negotiated her gum like an ocean navigator. Over her shoulder I could see the blonde scowling. "I'll see you, babe," said the car girl.

"Goodbye, Joanne," I said.

"Have you seen *A Question of Silence*?" the Smith girl was asking Naomi who had to admit that she'd missed that one.

"I liked *Presumed Innocent*," Naomi said and the Smith girl asserted that this was exactly the problem with Naomi's feminist consciousness.

At their table the car girl was squeezing the blonde around the waist until she screamed for her to stop. They had, both of them, gotten over me and it made me rather sad.

At the other end of the room, a lonely-looking woman about my age was dancing in the mirror with herself. She watched the women move around the bar like she was looking for a friend, and when she tried to meet their eyes they turned away or checked their watches or had another drink. She walked out alone at closing time behind me and Naomi and a Canadian truck driver who offered to do us both in the cab of her truck. We declined and I fell into bed back at the Lavender House as if I hadn't slept in days.

I woke up hung over in the middle of the night and thought I saw the dresser move. But Naomi was beside me in the bed. The room was dark as tar and pitch and the shade on the window closed out the light from the moon. I screamed and the door to our room opened up and slammed shut. In the light from the hall I saw a long blue robe and I heard the sound of feet running down the back stairs.

"What time is it?" Naomi sat up and rubbed her face. "What's wrong with you?" she said. "You look like you've just seen a ghost."

I told her I thought I had and I was going to take it up with Anya after breakfast.

XXX

Sam was busy putting the breakfast dishes away in her kitchen when we came around but she seemed happy for the company — at least Naomi's.

"We're looking for Anya," I said. "She wasn't at breakfast."

Sam shrugged. "Maybe she's around. Friday is her day off." She made eyes at Naomi and Naomi made them back.

"Mind if we check back in her room?" I asked.

Sam shrugged again. "Be my guest. It's down the hall, last door past the study."

"I'll stay here," Naomi said. She looked at me as

if it would be nice if I left sooner rather than later and I took the hint.

Sam's apartment was what would be called a railroad flat in Chicago. One long straight hall with rooms off to either side and either end like a barbell. Anya's room was in the back of Sam's apartment, through the kitchen, down the hall.

Anya wasn't there, so I let myself in. The room was big enough for a bed and a dresser squeezed in under a window opposite the door. When the house was built, this room was probably a pantry or a closet. Out the window I could see the big oak tree in Sam's backyard and a squad car parked across the street. It ruined the tableau and I looked at the photo of a woman in a gold frame on the dresser instead as it was better scenery.

It was the kind of picture that shows up in high school yearbooks and trade paperback authors' photos, with a studio-style black matte finish. A pretty black woman with perfect skin and hair so short you could see her scalp looked back at me and smiled, closed-mouthed. She had big brown eyes and the kind of head that could carry off female baldness. Whoever it was, it wasn't Hillela and I thought that was worth wondering about. When I put the photo back down on the dresser, Anya was watching me from the doorway.

"That's my lover, Claire." Anya had on a face that was all bunnies and kittens. She smiled at me like she didn't care I'd invited myself into her room and was putting fingerprints all over her picture. "She looks like you, don't you think?"

She did except with a better head and I told her so. But I was flattered that Anya had said it anyway. Anya was beautiful and it was nice to think you were the sort of thing that beautiful women might go for.

Anya answered my question without my having to ask. "Hillela was just for the summer. She knew it and it wasn't a problem. What she didn't like was Joan." Anya shrugged. "Hillela loves me." I agreed that pretty much summed it up, but I didn't like Anya taking it for granted. Self-sacrificing love is a rare commodity. I didn't like to see it wasted.

"So Hillela conveniently forgot to mention your side trip with Joan." I was getting the picture. "That's a pretty nice way to dismiss someone who loves you enough to lie by omission to the police." I didn't think Hillela deserved to get jerked around, even if she didn't mind it.

Anya shrugged again. "Life's a bitch." Her face was as bland as mashed potatoes. She said, "I could never be involved with a white woman long-term. Not that I'm a racist, but I need a lover who understands me. I can't imagine fighting the white world and then coming home and having to get into bed with it."

"You're on vacation now, though, right?" I shook my head. "Oh sure, I get it."

She narrowed her eyes. "The point," Anya said, "is that white women can no more banish their racism from their dealings with me than men can banish their sexism from dealings with women. In some cases it's just less damaging. Hillela tries to understand. She knows what it's like not to conform to the norms that western society says are good, but even she doesn't understand completely the nature of her privilege. If she let her hair grow and took out her women's symbol earrings she could get by unnoticed, no names, no friction. She could be doing mainstream comedy. You and I don't have that option."

She sat on the bed and ran her hands through her light brown hair. It was loose and falling in tiny waves around her face like a net. I wondered how much Anya knew about not conforming to the general ascetic of European beauty. I was the daughter my father said had gotten the brains while my straight-haired sister was the pretty one. It was hard to say whom the remark had damaged more as my sister Adeline would never believe that men could see her cleverness, now fifteen years later, and I was convinced that my lovers looked past my face and body to settle for a woman blessed with the faint praise of sparkling personality. "That was Joan's whole outing trip," Anya said. "Joan used to claim that the black civil rights movement was successful because black people couldn't closet themselves. Like if gays and lesbians couldn't closet themselves, we could have our own movement."

"The black civil rights movement isn't over," I said. "If you hadn't noticed, it's not a resounding success quite yet."

"You know, people think because I look like this, I must be stupid and they patronize me." Anya smiled at me down the bridge of her long thin nose. "I know there are still some problems in this country, that's why I could never commit myself to a white woman. It says too many conflicting things sociologically, you know."

"My girlfriend is white," I said.

The corners of her mouth made a little smile of pity. "Really?" she said, "and how's that going?"

"Not well." I had not intended myself to be an object lesson. "That's not the point," I said. "Our problems aren't really race related."

Anya pressed her lips together like closing her mouth was the only thing that could stop her from commenting. What she thought was that I was a woman with a bad case of self-hate and she was sorry for me. What I hoped was that I had simply fallen in love unwisely and things weren't working out. What I thought was, either way, it was none of her business.

"Let's talk about you," I said.

Anya shrugged her pretty shoulders. "What about me? I told you I was happy and I showed you why."

"What about Joan?" I asked her. "You say Hillela was summer entertainment, but I saw you at Herring Cove in the rain with Joan on Tuesday and it didn't look too much like uncomplicated recreational sex. Why don't you tell me what you were fighting about the day before she died."

Anya looked like she was sorry she'd been so friendly. She slipped the picture of Claire into a dresser drawer and closed it like show and tell was over.

"Look," I said, "I know you didn't tell the police about it and I'd just like a little private explanation so I don't feel like I have to. You could make it easy on me and make it easy on yourself," I said.

Anya knotted up her forehead. It made the only wrinkles in her perfect skin. "I'm sorry Joan's dead," she said after a while, "but I can't say I regret she's gone. She was blackmailing me. I told Hillela. That's part of what made Hillela so mad at Joan."

I asked what the other part was.

Anya shrugged like she figured the news was out. "The other thing that frosted Hillela was that I let Joan do it — blackmail me, that is. I'm not proud of it, but Joan wanted sex and I gave it to her when I didn't want to. Joan wouldn't have called it blackmail, of course. That was Hillela's word, and mine. Joan referred to it as reciprocation as in 'I'd like a little reciprocation, Anya,'" she mimicked Joan and her voice got angry. "You scratch my back and I'll scratch yours. The way of the world," Anya said like she wanted to change it.

I said it too: "The way of the world. What did she do for you?" I asked.

Anya sighed. She looked like someone had let the air out of her and her minimal tits seemed to sag on her chest. "I'm not very proud of that either," she said. "I announced I was a lesbian my freshman year when I met Claire and my parents cut off my money. So I sold term papers to get through school. I'm not proud of that either, but I didn't have many better alternatives. Anyway, Joan was in town doing a story on a hate crime against some gay students. She was a journalist, I wanted to be a journalist, and I was impressed. She'd worked at a lot of big papers before she started that free-lance gay activist thing. I thought I was networking and she thought I wanted her to hit on me." Anya looked at the floor and then back up at me. "Anyway, my side business was no secret except from the university administration. When Joan found out about me selling the papers, she started pressuring me to go

163

out with her. She was dealing with the administration all the time about the hate crimes incident and all. She was organizing the students, kind of an activist-at-large. Typically Joan, right?" Anya tried to smile, but failed. Her face made a grimace and her eyes clouded up. "Joan didn't threaten to say anything explicitly, but she let me know it would behoove me to keep her happy."

Anya wiped her nose on the back of her hand. "I'm applying to journalism schools in the fall and I couldn't take the chance she would talk to the administration. I could get expelled. I've got a light course load planned next year so I can work full time to pay the bills, but if it got out that I was helping people cheat it could crater my faculty recommendations for graduate school and forget about scholarships. Joan got me this job with Sam for the summer like she was doing me a favor. She said it would raise my consciousness, but mostly she just didn't like to think of me with Claire all summer. It wasn't like Joan was a satyr or something, she just wasn't what I wanted to do if I'd had the choice."

Anya stared at her hand for a while and when she looked back at me she was mad as hell. "All right, I hated her. But I didn't kill her and neither did Hillela. You know, I'm kind of glad the whole thing happened. It's like getting burned to find out the stove is hot. It taught me what a dirty fucked-up world this is."

I told her I was sorry. It was true.

"Don't be. I know you liked her." She smiled at the understatement as if I made her kind of sick. "I was watching you watch her. Let me tell you, for all the attitude she was throwing around, you weren't missing much. White girls are sometimes like that."

I stood up to go. "Thanks for the information," I said.

"Sure," said Anya. "If I find you in my room again, I'll be the one talking to the police."

XXXI

When I came down the hall I could see Naomi in profile, kissing Sam. They were pressed up against the kitchen counters; Naomi had managed to effect a kind of a flamingo swoon with a leg bent back and braced against the lower cabinets. One hand was lost in Sam's straight grey hair and the other was wrapped around her neck.

Beside the door between the kitchen and the hall I saw the board full of hooks where Sam kept the keys she used for cleaning. She and Naomi didn't look like they wanted to be disturbed so I put the ring in the pocket of my shorts and left. Since it was Anya's day off, I didn't imagine much housework was going to get done in the next day or so and I figured I could search the rooms when I wanted and get the keys back on the board by Friday after breakfast. If anyone noticed, I had a plan to drop the keys on the floor in the upstairs hall so Sam would think Anya had gotten careless.

The keys were heavy in my pocket as I strolled out to the porch. Shoplifters will tell you to walk in and out like you own the place. It's funny how things work.

Naomi didn't turn up for another half an hour. When she did she was red-faced and more self-satisfied than usual.

"Let's do some shopping," Naomi said, and I thought it was the best idea she'd had all day. I told her about Anya and the blackmail.

"Well, that's a motive, all right." Naomi's sandals made a thud on the hollow porch steps and their soles slapped the concrete walkway across the yard.

I opened the gate to the picket fence. "If Anya or Hillela did it, they did it together. That, or Anya snuck off from Hillela's in the middle of the night to wait for an opportunity to kill Joan." It seemed to me to violate the policeman's rule of simplicity. I said, "Besides, Joan's leverage over Anya was nothing new. Why kill her now? And anyway, I just don't think Anya's the kind of person to kill somebody — or Hillela either."

Naomi told me I was a sap. "People do what they have to do," she said.

I would have thought her lack of charity was a sad commentary on the state of the world, but I didn't have much time to think before a car came around the corner, cruising slowly, the way cab drivers troll off-rush-hour for fares. It was a squad car and Sheriff Harmon was in it.

He waved me over and rolled down the window.

The deputy driving was stony-faced, but Harmon himself was nice as pie to start.

"Ms. Kelly, I'm feeling lucky we caught you," Harmon said. But I didn't think luck had much to do with it. "I was hoping you'd have a minute to help us out." He pointed to Naomi. "You and your friend there," Harmon said and Naomi hunched her shoulders like she was trying to fade into the asphalt on the street. "You wouldn't happen to know anything about who Joan Di Maio might have been seeing —" He pulled out a notebook from his breast pocket and flipped through the pages, "— besides Sam Flynn and Anya Pendleton, would you?" Harmon smiled in my face. It was an awful display of coffee stains and shifted dental work. "I know we've asked you this before, Ms. Kelly, but we thought you might of had some time to think about it."

I told him I'd thought about it all I wanted to on Wednesday.

The deputy was smiling too now, a kind of a boys' club smirk and it was pissing me off. Harmon looked at him hard and he cut it out.

"We had a call," Harmon said. "From a woman who claimed you and Joan had a certain degree of intimacy." He tripped over the last word and started again in a way that seemed to make him feel better. "There's been some suggestion that you and Joan Di Maio were better friends than you've said to us and we wanted to give you the opportunity to clarify any misunderstanding."

"Who made the call?" Naomi had on her lawyer tone and for once I was glad to hear it.

Harmon looked out the car windshield and then

167

down at the lint on his pants. He smiled. "I'm afraid it would be unprofessional for me to say."

"Wait a second." I made a mental note to add kissing and telling to the ever growing list of Joan's venial sins. "Do you mean to tell me you people came all the way over here to hassle me over some gossip, after you tied me up all Wednesday morning of my vacation and all I've been trying to do is what's right? You know, I could have just left her there and saved myself a world of trouble."

Naomi cut her eyes at me, but it was no use. The ugly tone in my voice was doing my soul some good. "Listen Harmon, I told you people everything I knew on Wednesday."

Harmon took a breath and let it out. "Ms. Kelly, we are very sorry to have inconvenienced you. But you'll have to understand we have a murder here. It's a serious business — murder." He stepped on the word and stared at me as if he were deciding for himself whether I was up to it. "And we have to follow every possible lead to its conclusion. So we thought in light of the information we've received, you might want to amend your statement. We'd appreciate your cooperation."

"I don't think Virginia here wants to be uncooperative, Officer." Naomi sounded like she was trying to talk her way out of a traffic ticket. It didn't seem to be working. "Do you, Ginny?" Naomi said.

I said, "What I don't want is to be harassed on my vacation. And another thing, Harmon," I said, "quit following me."

Harmon took another breath and made a note in his pad. "All right. If that's the way you want to play it, Ma'am, we won't hold you up here any longer. If you find there's anything else you'd like to tell us though, you know where we are."

"Thank you, sir," Naomi's expression was plastic.

Harmon looked me square in the eyes again. "I think the best thing you can do right now, Miss, is to cooperate. That's a piece of good advice." What it was, was a threat. "By the way," he said, "we'd appreciate it if you wouldn't go anywhere for awhile."

The deputy leered at me again before he put the car in gear. He kicked up gravel pulling off the curb.

"I have to get inside," Naomi said, "I'm going to be sick." She looked wrung out and angry. "Let me give you another piece of good advice, Virginia: don't call the police by their last names."

But I thought they had gone beyond what was appropriate shake-down etiquette. "Look, shaking me down on the street wasn't exactly polite. Somebody planted a gun in our room and called the police so they could find it there. And when that didn't work, whoever it was called the cops and told them Joan and I were an item. Now the police say I can't leave here. Somebody is trying to pin this murder on me and it's somebody who has access to this house."

I said, "Look, whoever killed Joan knew where she would be at five-thirty in the morning. It wasn't someone she picked up because you said she left the bar alone."

"She left the bar with me," Naomi said. "I didn't kill her."

But I figured whoever did had to be watching the house from either the inside or the outside. If Joan had followed her usual routine, it could be anyone, but she had run two hours earlier than usual. So whoever it was had either stood outside all night waiting for an opportunity or somehow knew that she was running early.

"That means it's got to be somebody at the guest house." Naomi counted on her fingers. "Either Anya, Helen, or that Barb and her girlfriend, what's-her-name."

"Or Sam," I said. "Let's be thorough, all right?"

"All right," Naomi said. "But why leave a note to explain a crime of passion? Like I said before, if Joan deserved to have a handgun put in her face, she didn't need a note from Sam to tell her about it."

I thought she had a point. "Just asking," I said, but I was getting some other uncharitable thoughts. "So, what was it like kissing Sam after all these years?"

"Sam and I getting back together doesn't have a thing to do with who killed Joan." Naomi was red-faced again and I had to admit I liked seeing her that way. Her being off balance for a change instead of me.

"She was nice enough to get killed and remove herself as an impediment to your happiness, though." I smiled. "You owe her your thanks." Naomi in that selfless state called love seemed both sweet and totally unbelievable. I told her so and she remarked that I was full of shit.

"No, really," I said. "I really want to know. What's it like in reruns?"

Naomi smoothed down the back of her hair. "It was just like coming home." She managed to say it without cracking a smile. "So what are we going to do about our other problem, smart girl?"

I took the room keys out of my pocket and tossed them in the air. "I'm still thinking, but I'm getting ideas."

"I know what you're thinking and you'd better stop it." Naomi looked at the keys in my open palm like they made her ill, but she wasn't altogether convincing and she started talking louder to make up for it. "If you're going to do anything illegal I don't want to know about it." She covered her ears with her hands. "All right?" She said, "I can't be encouraging this kind of thing."

"What kind of thing?" I said. "I'm going for a walk upstairs. So, why don't you go keep Sam company for a while? If anybody comes along you just let me know."

"I can't know about this," Naomi said, "okay?"

"Okay," I said. "Relax."

"All right." Naomi ducked her head and opened up her hands. "I'm not saying this is all right with me, but if anybody comes, I'll whistle. See?" She whistled through the gap in her teeth. "And if you get caught doing something I haven't said that I condone, my advice is to say the door was open and you were curious about how the other rooms were decorated." Naomi combed her fingers through the hair at the crown of her head. "Offer to show whoever our room. But I don't think you ought to let me know about this, okay?"

I said, "I'd better not get caught. That's what I think."

"Of course not." Naomi shrugged. "That's what

I've been saying." She slapped me on the back. "If I was going to break the law I'd start with Joan's room and see if the police missed anything." Naomi walked off towards Sam's apartment. She didn't bother looking back.

XXXII

There was no one in the hall. The door to Joan's room opened easily and I closed it behind me. Someone had boxed up some of her things and left them sitting on the mattress of her bed. Aside from that the room looked almost lived in. A hairbrush that had not been packed lay bristles down on the dresser and the manuscript of her book was on the card table where she'd worked. The furniture tops were clean except for fingerprint powder the police had left and there was nothing in the waste baskets. I figured their contents had gone with Sheriff Harmon along with the sheets on the bed. The lady in blue still hung on the wall with her lips in a thin tight smile and fat white cats playing in the lap of her dress. She gave me the creeps. I turned her portrait face-down on the bed and left.

Helen Bowen's room was the next one down the hall. I knocked on the door, put the key in the lock and left the door ajar so I could credibly say I'd found it open.

The room was neat and I thought I would prefer Helen to Naomi as a roommate. I opened the bottom drawer of the dresser and ran my hands under the clothing. There was a battery-operated vibrator under the socks. In the underwear was a small spiral notebook. I took it to the dressing table and opened it from the back. The last entry was dated July 22 in thin looped writing. It read: *"It's over — what I've come here to do and now I feel so aimless you cannot imagine. I will stay here until Friday to rest. Then I can go anywhere and not worry again."*

I kept reading backwards through the entries until I came to one that stopped my heart. *"Tonight you die."* I read it over and over again until I heard footsteps outside the door. I left the book on the dresser and hunkered down behind the bed. I was worried the pounding in my chest would give me away until I saw that it was just Naomi.

She closed the door behind her before she picked up the notebook on the dressing table. "Ginny? Have you seen this?" Naomi read from the book aloud. " '. . *I've waited a long time to see you and have my retribution.'* Goddamn," she said. "Will you check this out."

I got up from behind the bed and told her I already had.

"We've hit the jackpot." Naomi waved the book around. She sat down on the bed. "This is some extremely deep shit."

I asked her what we were going to do and she tightened up her forehead. "The short answer is, I think if we match the writing in this diary with the note from the murder site we'll have ourselves a murderer. The long answer is we need a story to get this diary to the police." She rubbed her hand against her hairline. "Give me the key. All the keys while you're at it." Naomi put the keys in her pocket. "The door was open, right?"

I frowned. "Well, no. I used the key."

"Don't be stupid," Naomi said. "The door was open, right? It was ajar." She opened the door lock in the knob with a kleenex and stood back to look at it from a distance with satisfaction. "Right?" Naomi said again.

I shrugged. "Okay."

Naomi walked around the room. "The door was ajar. And you are a private citizen." She was in her element.

"All right," I said, "but I can't see what you're getting at."

"I'm getting your story straight, potato head. Do you think we're going to sashay into the cops without a reasonable explanation? Not that they'll believe it." Naomi closed her eyes and thought. "But that won't matter. It'll take the heat off you. If we work it right, Harmon will just lock Helen up and thank us in his prayers."

"We broke into this woman's room," I pointed out. "Don't you think that's kind of a problem?"

Naomi puffed up her cheeks and blew the air out hard. "The door was open," she repeated, talking very slowly. "And you were curious as to how the other rooms were furnished. God," Naomi said. "No one would argue that. Ours is a fucking museum. You walked in the room thinking Helen was in and when she wasn't you looked around thinking she couldn't be far away. The diary was out and you beat a trail down to the police station after you read it, civic-minded creature that you are."

"Are you sure this is going to be okay?" I was doubtful.

Naomi rubbed her hands together. "Well, it will be if you don't change your story during the trial. Who says lesbians aren't good citizens?"

"What trial?"

"Of course you'll have to testify. You found the notebook. Relax, Ginny. It'll be out of town. Besides you and I are never going to be president." Naomi crossed her legs above the knees of her bermuda shorts. "Then again, I might. So, I think it's better that you do the testifying."

I told her I didn't think the Republican nomination was close enough for her to worry about.

"I was in our room taking a nap, when you woke me up to show me this." Naomi patted my cheek. "Remember? I was the one who told you you had to go to the police."

"Why can't we just send it anonymously?" I said. "I broke into this woman's room to get this."

"*You* broke into this room. Don't say *we*." Naomi said, "That's the problem with the world today. Nobody's ever willing to get involved."

"You'd better think of another way to get this thing to Harmon. Because I'm not going to lie under oath. That's for damn sure," I said.

"Hello in there," said Helen Bowen. Her frizzy-permed hair hung around her head like angel-hair netting and her face was so red from the sun, it looked like it hurt.

175

Naomi looked at me and whistled through the gap in her teeth. Too little too late.

"Been to the beach?" I explained, "The door was open and we were just admiring your room."

"Were you?" Helen took her beach bag off her shoulder and let it hang at the end of her arm. It hit the floorboards with a kind of a metallic thud. "Do you like it?"

"Lots," Naomi said. "We both love antiques." She dropped the diary behind her back like a sideshow magician.

"Have a seat." Helen gave the bed a pat with her open hand. "Take a load off." She took a damp towel out of her beach bag and hung it over the wicker love seat by the window. "I love this old wicker." The sides of her mouth worked up in a sad little smile and she bent over to rummage through her bag on the seat of the little couch. "Oh sit down, please."

"We really can't. We have to go," Naomi said. "Ginny, let's go." I saw her slip the notebook in the pocket of her bermuda shorts before we headed for the door. So did Helen.

"Oh have a seat anyway." Helen patted the bed again. "Sit, sit," she said as if it were an invitation to a tea party, but she'd taken up a small black revolver from her bag. As far as I was concerned, it put her sincerity into question, but I told her I thought we'd stay since she'd asked so nicely. I dropped myself on the bed; the box springs thumbed and creaked and Naomi's face looked like warm death under her tan.

"You, too." Helen made a wide sweeping motion with her arm that ended in the business end of the gun. She pointed it at Naomi and she sat down too. "And sit so I can see your hands, please. Put them on your laps." Then she took the cane-seated chair from in front of the dressing table and sat down across from us, bracing the arm that held the gun between her side and the arm of the chair. "I think we should talk."

"I couldn't agree with you more," Naomi said. "You're in a world of trouble."

"Shut up." Helen had lost her smile.

"Come on, Helen," Naomi said. "You're not going to get away with this. The cops are watching this house, so how are you going to get away? Why don't you just give me the gun and shorten the amount of time you're going to have to do."

"Shut up," Helen said again.

I had developed a dull but persistent headache and it felt like my brain was being squeezed out my ears. "Shut up, will you, Naomi," I said. "We've got some real problems here."

"That's an understatement, if I've ever heard one." Helen giggled from somewhere in her gut. Her whole body shook and only the hand with the gun was steady against the arm of the chair. "In a couple of days I would have been gone from here, but you had to come digging around my room. Do you think I wanted this kind of trouble?"

"Well, you do have a gun," Naomi was saying. "You make your bed and you lay in it."

Helen smiled. "That's what I always say. You make your bed." She didn't finish the sentence.

"I'll scream," Naomi said. "And you'll regret that, I promise you will."

"Do you think I want to have this gun?" Helen

ran her hand through her hair as if she planned to take it out at the roots.

"Shut up, Naomi," I said. "Of course you don't want that nasty gun, Helen. I know you don't. And you don't want to hurt us. You just had to do what you had to do. I can respect that. I can understand you've been wronged."

"Don't patronize me." Helen wagged the gun like it was an extension of her finger. "You've no idea what I've been through."

"What did I tell you." Naomi cursed under her breath. "For Godsakes, she can't shoot both of us," Naomi said. "I'm going to scream."

"Shut up," I said. "I think we might be able to work this out between us, Helen."

"Oh shut up," Helen groaned, "she's right." She laid the gun on her knee and sighed as if she'd done a hard day's work. "I can't shoot you both although I could hurt one of you badly enough." Helen laughed. "If I shot either one of you, it'd bring the cops right down around my ears. I'm in a box, but desperate people do crazy things. What we all need is for you to forget about this. Put that diary you've got in your pocket on the bed or I promise I will shoot you, Naomi. Would you like to hear a story?" Helen didn't really ask.

"All right." I thought it might buy us some time.

She settled back into the chair like she wanted to be listened to. "Then tell her to put the diary on the bed." She pointed the gun with a purpose. "It doesn't belong to her. Tell her to put it down and we can talk about this."

"Put the book down, will you?" I thought if Helen

would put the gun away my head might stop pounding.

"I'm going to scream," Naomi said. It sounded like a promise.

Helen sighed. She looked at me and opened her arms. "If she says another word, I don't care what happens, I'll shoot your friend. Right now just to have some peace."

"Oh, have it your way then." Naomi tossed the notebook onto the bed and Helen let the gun rest again on her thigh.

The noise between my ears went down a few hundred decibels and I was thankful.

Helen closed her eyes and sighed again through her nose. When she opened her eyes they were watery and tired. "This whole revenge thing has just about worn me out," she said. "You know, I didn't deserve this kind of grief. I was the youngest associate judge in the history of downstate Illinois, daughter of an electric company lineman married to a junior congressman." She took a flask from the side of her bag and raised it up in a kind of salute. "Then I made the circuit court and I felt just like Cinderella." Helen took a drink and held the flask out. "Do you want some?"

Naomi shook her head. "No thank you. I'm a little sick to my stomach. You understand."

I took the flask and had a belt as I thought it was going to be my last. The rum went down my throat like liquid fire and the heartburn it gave me took my mind off more serious problems for a while.

"I had a husband and a child and I had women lovers, many." Helen smiled. "Are you surprised? I wanted respectability and renown and I wanted my own way too and I had it. It wasn't a bad existence. My benefactor died and I was elected acting judge to the circuit court."

She brought the flask out again and this time kept it for herself. "My husband was very rich from several generations of agri-business so he never went near a tractor. He put on a homespun routine for the papers, of course, but he really didn't like his hands to get dirty. He studied law and aspired to politics. He married me because I was smart and rural and cloth-coat common without being too plain to take out. He had ambitions and ideas. Like Nelson Rockefeller, Roger thought he ought to be president with his big ideas. When his father sat him down and told him that they bought politicians in his family, they didn't become them, Roger just wouldn't believe it. The old man finally gave up and funded Roger's campaigns after he lost his first couple of elections. The old man couldn't bear to see him lose. Money always wins. I learned that early on in life. I married Roger out of law school because he was rich and I was happy to let his family buy me my associate judgeship. I was happy in general not to be married to a man who worked for the light company. Roger didn't disgust me."

Helen giggled. It was a nervous sound and it started and stopped independent of her words like a bad case of hiccups. "Well he didn't thrill me, mind you, but I had my girls' nights out." She smiled to herself, remembering. "On one of those nights, I met Joan Di Maio at a women's bar. She recognized me, she said, from the local papers. Joan looked up to my position and I was flattered. Women didn't generally recognize me at the bars. I went with her to where she was living. More than once and she whispered in my ears how she had haunted the bars trying to meet me. She said she loved to think how powerful I was. I think her first intention was to network and then things progressed. I can be charming when I want to be. It's charming to have a young woman so interested in you." Helen waved her hand. "But let me tell you what happened and we'll get to that."

"Do you mind if I smoke?" Naomi took her cigarettes and her lighter from the front pockets of her shorts.

"Yes, I suppose this might be your last opportunity for that." Helen began to giggle again, more nervous than amused. "I'm sorry. This is my first attempt at confinement."

"Can I open a window?" I thought if Naomi screamed someone might hear her. I thought we could start a fire and escape. I thought of a lot of crazy things like whether or not I had told Em that I loved her.

"Don't even think about moving, dear." Helen's face stiffened up. "I think we'll make do the way we are."

It took Naomi both hands to light her cigarette. She laid her lighter on the bedspread beside her afterwards and let smoke drift out of her open mouth in rings.

Helen said, "Throw the lighter on the floor by me now. You'd be surprised how hard it is to get things to burn and you'll just make me angry with you."

I tossed the lighter underhanded at the leg of Helen's chair. My palms were soaked and the pits of my arms smelled unpleasantly like fear. The single clear thought in my head was that I would probably not ever see Em again, and that the irrevocable end of my relationship might be the product of this strange unforeseeable twist of circumstance. It left me with an odd sense of numbed relief that things had passed so completely beyond my control like the sigh of your muscles when a heavy weight can finally be shrugged off and dropped.

Helen kicked the lighter under her chair with the heel of her sandals and I watched it skid along the wood well out of my reach.

"I slept with Joan weekly for three months which is more than my usual routine with women," Helen was saying. "But it was casual. I won't tell you that I was in love with her. I have my needs and they were getting serviced. I was fond of her, of course." Helen had let the gun droop in her hand so it pointed towards her foot. She shored it up again. "I guess that's neither here nor there. I just want you to know I wasn't planning a crime of passion. I liked the way she looked up to me and of course I liked the way she looked. That was that. Sex is cheap, but adoration is hard to come by and Joan was so convinced that in the position I held I could do some good for people that I almost began to believe it myself." Helen watched Naomi taste the smoke on her tongue. "Let me have a hit of that, will you?"

"Do I have a choice?" Naomi said.

"No," Helen giggled. "I don't suppose you do." She brought both her hands out to take the cigarette, the empty one and the one with the gun behind hit. In her hand the gun looked big and dangerous, and its nose was long and thin like a movie western six-shooter. Helen looked pleased when the transfer went uneventfully and she held the cigarette lightly between her thumb and index fingers, puffing on it and blowing the smoke immediately out in front of her. "I haven't smoked since I was seventeen years old."

Helen handed Naomi back her cigarette and sighed. She said, "It happened that I was working on a case that involved three students from the state college. The State and the Defense had agreed on a bench trial halfway through. There was a chalk board up in the student union called the First Amendment Board, something like that. Students wrote whatever they liked on it. The idea was to cut down on campus graffiti, but the gay and lesbian student group had decided it was a way to combat what Joan used to call invisibility. I laughed the first time she said that to me and I asked her what she could possibly hope to gain from being seen. Joan was an idealist. Anyway, one of the students was a friend of hers, that is, they belonged to the same activist group and he was writing pro-gay slogans on the board one day when two other students were writing slurs. A fight broke out and all the boys were roughed up. The straight ones broke the gay one's ribs and the gay one broke one of their noses. No one was badly hurt, but they traded charges. The gay student's organization asserted that this was a hate crime. Of course, it was simply a brawl."

"Sure." Naomi said. "I remember that case now."

"Do you?" Helen shook her head. "You're so full of shit. No one gives a damn about the hate crimes statute except left-wing gays and minorities. The case was a non-event as far as I or anybody else was concerned. It wasn't even a hate crime. It was a silly case and I was the judge. The gay student got nine months court supervision for battery and I gave the others the same sentence. Joan was very disappointed; she'd been lobbying me between the sheets for weeks. The sex stopped after the sentencing, but I didn't care. Joan was an uncomplicated relationship. It's hard to get hooked on a woman with no mystery." Helen contemplated this. "But, of course, her adoration was engaging."

Naomi grunted.

"Don't you agree?" Helen jiggled the heel of the gun on her knee. "My foot fell asleep," she said. "Where was I?"

I said, "It's hard to get hooked on a woman with no mystery."

"We don't deserve to be bored to death," Naomi said. "Will you please shoot us or get to the point."

Helen smiled in spite of herself. "All right," she said. "After the straight boys didn't get the kind of time that people who wanted an example made of them were asking, she went away. Our parting was more sad than venomous. I had not lived up to her vision of me. Life goes on. We bought my son a pony for his seventh birthday and Roger thought he was in the pool of vice-presidential hopefuls. I took another lover, an associate from Roger's firm; and I will tell you she was lovely. Of course, that is neither here nor there.

"I was a cinch to be reaffirmed until Joan outted me in her weekly newspaper column, in letters to the circuit court and to outsiders running for my spot. The battery case became a small-time scandal, manageable for anybody but the ambitious wife of a junior congressman. Of course, my ethics were called into question — sleeping with an interested party regardless of gender was ill-advised. There was adultery since I was married and there was lesbianism. It was ugly."

"I can imagine," I said.

"Can you?" said Helen. "I really doubt that. My husband left me as a matter of course. Not that he hadn't known I was a dyke, not that he even minded, but he had his reputation to think of. It was a friendly parting and I didn't especially mind except he took my son and him I miss. His grandparents tell him things about me I don't want to repeat."

"I'm sorry," I said. "Do you ever see your son?"

Helen shook her head. "That was part of the settlement. I couldn't work anymore and I had to live, so I sold my rights to him. Money always wins. It took me a year to hit bottom and another year to get back to sea level. Joan had gained from my troubles. She's risen through the activist ranks and got her own column. Oh, she was very busy." Helen nodded and frowned. "I read the gay papers so I could follow what she was doing, where she was. And when I got ready, I went looking for her."

I remembered, then, Sam had told me before breakfast on Sunday that she was booked for the week, and I wished I'd remembered it earlier. I said to Helen, "So you left the note under Joan's door and told me you were waiting for a room, but of course you'd booked the room already." I'd known enough to figure at least part of it out all along, but

I hadn't; and it had put me and Naomi in this mess we were in. "I'm sorry," I said to Naomi.

Helen was cheerful and full of information. "It was true, the part that I'd followed Joan from Boston, but I wanted to get the lay of the land before I checked in here. So I waited until Tuesday. And when you recognized me Wednesday, I thought you knew."

"I didn't. Did you sign your name?" I asked. I had developed a curiosity in the face of what I saw was probable death.

"I signed my first name," Helen said. "But I don't think Joan connected with it. Joan had made herself into a minor celebrity out of my scandal and there were always women around. I didn't leave any number, no way to get in touch with me."

Helen was giggling again in fits and starts. "It's funny, I thought I wanted to play with her mind a little, but when I saw her again at the bar I just wanted to kill her. Maybe it was just a little vanity to think she ought to have remembered me. I would have liked a drink of that gin she was offering women in the room for old time's sake. I wasn't unfond of her, you know. But Naomi was there in my place, weren't you, Naomi? Don't lie, I followed you home from the Waterfront. I thought my note would ensure that she was walking home alone, but it didn't. So, I think that makes Naomi and I the last ones to see poor little Joan alive — besides whoever killed her. And of course Sam. Sam saw you come in too. I waited until you two got inside. When I came in Sam was sitting in the parlor in the dark just staring out the windows."

I was staring myself — but at Naomi. "You slept

with Joan the night before she died and didn't bother to tell me?" I would have felt worse about it, if I hadn't felt so cheap myself.

"I'll explain it to you later when we're out of here," Naomi said.

"Don't bother. I don't know when that's going to be. Anyway, I've got a pretty good idea what's going on now. Thanks a lot," I said. "That's pretty chickenshit, Naomi."

"Isn't it though." Helen smiled strangely for a second before the muscles in her mouth went slack. "I was listening at the wall between our rooms. It sounded like Naomi had a pretty good time."

"I've had better." Naomi folded her arms. "Can we just cut to the chase?"

"That's fine with me," Helen said. "I listened and then I sat up in my room waiting for her to come out. I do embroidery. It calms my nerves and I've learned to do such beautiful things. I'd love to show you, but maybe we'll save it for another time." Helen said, "I knew, of course, that it would pay to wait. Joan is a creature of habit."

"Was," Naomi said stiffly.

"Of course. Sometimes I forget." Helen inclined her head. "Joan was a creature of habit," she went on, "and I knew she wouldn't miss her morning run for a woman."

Naomi coughed. She put out her cigarette on the sole of her sandal.

Helen took a drink from her flask. "Joan and I were alike that way, self-contained. Sex is a little vacation from our genuine passions. Mine of course was my ambition. Hers was her self-image. She liked to see herself reflected in other people's admiration.

187

It was better than a mirror, although she loved those too. But women augmented her reputation. And Joan wanted so much to be a legend, but she could take you or leave you, really. Did it disappoint you, Naomi," Helen said, "to wake up and find she loved jogging more than she liked touching you? Don't take it personally, dear; she'd planned to run early so you wouldn't know."

Naomi clenched her teeth. I watched the vanity rise up in her face like bile.

Helen wrinkled her nose. "I'm glad to see it's not over Joan that we're having this trouble."

"What did you do when you heard her go out?" I asked.

"That's just the point, I fell asleep. They just kept going on and on in there. But I'd set my travel alarm for seven because I figured you'd have snuck back to your room by then." Helen yawned as if she was getting sleepy. "Joan ran down Commercial Street to the beach and back the same way every day, past the abandoned construction site. But when I went to wait for her there, she was already dead. And of course, when I thought about it, it wasn't really surprising. In thirty years Joan had probably made a phenomenal number of enemies. But at that point she was like a wall full of graffiti. I couldn't stand not to put my two cents in so I wrote the note and stuck it in her pocket so it wouldn't blow away. It was a pretty trucky business to get it done without stepping in the blood. But I managed it. Then I left her for someone else to find and counted my blessings."

"So, what are you going to do now?" I said.

"That depends on you," said Helen. "A lot of

things could happen at this juncture. We could all walk out of here and have a drink down at Jocelyn's." Helen laid the gun on her lap. "We could all have a nice rest of our lives if you gave me that notebook. After all, I didn't do it."

It didn't seem to me like much of a story. "Wait a second. You stalked Joan for years and we're supposed to believe somebody else killed her first?"

"I think she has a point, Ginny." Naomi held the book in her palm. "We could burn the book and all walk out of here like pals."

"That's right." Helen was hopeful. "We could all be friends."

Naomi rolled her eyes. "Not too damn likely." She tucked the book in her back pocket and stood up. "Maybe the cops will believe you, but I don't and I'm going to go now. Stand up, Ginny," she said. "We're going."

"I didn't shoot Joan but I could have. I could shoot you both to survive," Helen said, but her voice was weak. "What would you do if someone took away everything you'd ever thought of having and didn't care?"

I didn't know what I would do if someone took away my job at Whytebread out of selfish ambition and for personal aggrandizement, and then cynically twisted the politics of our community to justify it. I hoped I wouldn't get a gun, but I wasn't so sure. I could see what she was saying, but what's right is right.

"Stand the fuck up, Virginia," Naomi said.

I felt my stomach turn.

"You know, she revelled in it," Helen said. "Listen, she benefited from it. She wrote a weekly column expressly so she could bring this pain on other people. Who cares who killed her, anyway? Let's just let it lie."

"I'm sorry." I stood up, watching Naomi move closer to the door by inches. I envied her progress.

Helen was whining pitiably. "I didn't kill her. But no one's going to believe me now. I was a prosecutor. I know that." She watched my feet working their way along the floor in baby steps behind Naomi's. "Are you really going to give my diary to the police?" Helen asked, but she didn't move from her chair and her gun was lying across her lap. Out of the corner of my eye I saw her raise it to her head.

I could hear my feet shuffling against the oak and I felt my toes on the threshold of the door. With another step, I knew I could be standing outside.

The room was very quiet when the gun went off. By the time I hit the floor, Naomi was already off and running. I listened to the sound of her feet, along the hall and down the stairs. She had left Helen's journal laying on the runner in the hall. The light from the window caught the shiny silver spirals.

XXIII

I closed the door to Helen's room very softly and caught up to Naomi downstairs in the parlor. Sam and the women from Vermont had gathered around the couch in kind of a carnival atmosphere. Loud Barb and her girlfriend were wearing matching sun visors that said Arthur Andersen & Co. on them and Sam wore another pair of her bright cotton pants, but they looked garish to me after the events of the last hour. Naomi had draped herself in their admiration and she was taking credit for solving Joan's murder single-handedly.

"Well, I knew it had to be Helen," Naomi was saying. "I knew it instinctively." She looked at me and smiled. "Didn't I tell you yesterday, Virginia? You have to know people in this business."

"I never liked that Helen," Loud Barb said. "I think she wanted Jane." She squeezed her girlfriend for emphasis and I almost laughed until I looked over and saw the diamond ring on Sam's hand. It was the diamond I'd seen on her hand in the kitchen Wednesday morning. And I remembered that it was the same one Joan had worn. I'd seen it at the Waterfront the night before she died but it was missing when I'd found the body. And I thought that things were finally starting to make sense. Helen's story about the note and Sam sitting by herself all night in the dark.

I remembered Naomi had told me that Joan was

killed with an automatic weapon like the one I'd found in our room, a square-looking thing, but the gun on the floor of the bedroom where Helen had shot herself was a revolver that looked like something out of a movie western. And for someone who just wanted to be left in peace it didn't make much sense for Helen to be phoning the police encouraging them to search the Lavender House before she could slip out of town.

"It must have been just harrowing for you," the quiet woman said to Naomi who was trying to look very brave.

"Well, you just have to know people." Naomi was about ready to launch into her story again when I had to stop her.

"Wait a second, Naomi," I said. "We've got a problem here." I told the quiet woman to go call the police.

"The phone's in the kitchen," said Sam. "Ask for Harmon directly. He'll like the name recognition."

"Sorry about that, Ginny." Naomi dropped down in the reading chair and rubbed the side of her face. "I know I should have called them. But, look, I couldn't face the cops right away. I was hoping we could just close up the room and wait half an hour until my stomach has a chance to calm down before we have to call Harmon out here. I promise you he's going to be a pill. We might as well have our ducks in order. God," she said. "Isn't Helen dead? I didn't think to check."

"She's dead, all right. But Helen didn't kill Joan." I said. "Sam did."

"Oh, my," said Loud Barb. The quiet woman

opened her mouth very wide then clapped her palm over her lips so no sound got out.

"You're nuts," said Sam.

I didn't think so. It was just an educated guess, but it made sense to me. "You killed Joan, didn't you," I said to Sam. "You're wearing the ring I saw on Joan before she died. It wasn't on the body when I found it and now it's on your hand."

"My God, I think it is," the quiet woman said. "Will you look at that, Barb?" She squeezed her girlfriend's arm.

Sam stood up from the couch. "I don't know what you're talking about."

I told her we'd let the police sort it out and she didn't look pleased — neither did Naomi.

Sam crossed her arms. "Will you tell your friend she's crazy, Naomi," she said.

I said, "Helen was just a lucky coincidence. She was going to kill Joan, but you beat her to it. You killed Joan and you took the antique ring because you couldn't bear to lose it. You couldn't afford to draw attention to yourself by going down to the police station to claim it. It's such a little thing I guess you didn't think anyone would notice. But think about it," I said to Naomi. "If Helen was going to kill herself anyway, why not admit she'd killed Joan before she died? She couldn't even shoot you, Naomi, and God knows you're annoying as hell. Why would she admit to the note but not the shooting if it wasn't true?"

Naomi frowned and I kept talking up my theory. "Sam was in a box with Joan. She couldn't stop her from sleeping around right under her nose which had to be humiliating and she couldn't kick her out or Joan would start writing columns about her high-profile guests. Sam saw Naomi come home with Joan the night before she died and that was the last straw — Naomi and Joan together."

I looked at Sam on the couch. "You stayed up all night and when Joan went out to run in the dark, you waited for her near the construction site. Maybe you were going to confront her; maybe you did. But whatever happened you had a gun with you and you shot her."

The only thing I wasn't sure of was why Sam didn't look very nervous; it was making me unsure of the whole house of cards.

In fact, Sam looked like she might yawn. "That's all speculation. I'd like to see you prove it. But you can't, because it's nuts."

"I don't think so." I held my ground, but I felt like the lone voice in the wilderness. I said, "You shot Joan and then you tried to make the police think I did it by stashing the gun in our room after Joan told you she and I had slept together." But after I'd said it, I thought it made my story sound even more unhinged.

"You slept with Joan?" Naomi looked up and slapped her forehead. "I thought you told me you didn't sleep with her."

"I lied," I said. "So now we're even."

The women from Vermont had their heads going back and forth like two people at a fast-paced tennis match and they looked like they were enjoying the game. I would have liked to be able to say the same, but the truth was I thought I might be losing.

"You're crazy." Sam stretched her lips across her teeth in something that was trying to pass for amusement but then she gave it up. "Why would Joan tell me she'd slept with you?"

I was afraid I was going to have to admit she had a point. But all of a sudden Loud Barb's girlfriend started talking and she wouldn't shut up.

"I don't think Virginia's crazy at all." The quiet woman was shaking her head. "I remember that diamond distinctly now because Barb and I were admiring Joan's ring ourselves at breakfast, weren't we Barb?"

Loud Barb bounced her head up and down while her girlfriend talked.

"The ring Joan was wearing was exactly the ring you have on now, Sam. Joan even told me you gave it to her and of course I said I would love it if Barb gave me something like that. It's so old and solid, and of course it's platinum." The quiet woman, Jane, looked at Sam's ring like she wanted to make an offer on it right there. "We love estate jewelry, don't we Barb," the quiet woman said.

Loud Barb stopped her head mid-nod. "Forget the jewelry for a minute, honey. What I want to now is when did that Joan have time to tell you all that?" Loud Barb looked stricken.

The quiet woman blushed. "I stopped by her room one afternoon to hear about her book when you were taking a nap. I'd run into her in the hall and she offered me a drink. Of course I didn't have one since it was before four in the afternoon, but I did want to hear about the book." She blushed again and then looked hard at Sam. "You should know,

Joan and I shared some very special time. She told me you loved that ring, Sam, and you gave it to her because you loved her too."

Sam looked at the ring. "I did love Joan." She sounded as if she was going to cry and Naomi cut her eyes at me.

Loud Barb kept asking her girlfriend what else Joan had loved and if looks could have killed I thought we might have had another murder.

The quiet woman said, "Oh there was nothing between Joan and me but the kinship of artists. But you know, I myself have dabbled in poetry." The quiet woman had pulled herself up like some old Hollywood movie diva and her speech was sounding more and more like studio melodrama with every word. "As much as I like you Sam, I think I need to come forward with this information in Joan's memory. She did so many things for the community, you know. I think it's what she would have wanted — justice."

"That's a wonderful sentiment." Sam was really crying now and Naomi looked like she was going to hit me. "But I guess Joan didn't tell you that I asked for the ring back the day before she died. That's why I have it. Virginia saw us fighting in the kitchen. Things weren't working out and I asked for it back. She gave it back. That's the end of the story. I haven't wanted to remember the bad times," Sam said. "I don't think that's very hard to understand."

It wasn't and I felt like a heel even though I couldn't figure out when Joan could have given the ring back. Since Naomi'd left the bar with Joan and stayed with her until she'd sneaked off to jog and gotten killed.

"I think I'd apologize if I were you." Naomi was frowning so hard I thought it would take her years to get rid of the lines. "There's a woman upstairs with a diary all full of death wishes and I don't think you can prove anything with regard to some ring you think you saw, Virginia." I knew it was trouble when Naomi used my full name. She said, "Sam asked for the ring back and she got it back, that's all." Naomi smiled as if she'd just told me where I got off and I thought she probably had.

"I'm awfully sorry," I said to Sam and she smiled at me as if all was forgiven even if it looked like Naomi was going to hold a grudge.

"You're some fucking friend," Naomi growled at me.

"Now, everybody's tired." Sam dried her eyes. "Everybody's under stress. I think we ought to forget this happened. The police will be here soon and this will all be over. Poor Helen." She put her feet up on the coffee table by the couch like it was nice to take a load off.

Naomi was still shooting me nasty looks.

"Oh my God," the quiet woman said again. She was looking at Sam's shoes. When I looked for myself my mouth dropped open.

"What's wrong?" Sam was watching us watch her and it looked like someone had painted the soles of her tennis shoes the color of Georgia clay. The treads were stained brick red. "What's wrong," she said again and all I could do was point to her shoes. There were white parts and there were reddish-brown parts; and I was pretty sure the reddish-brown parts were dried up blood.

"How come there's blood on the bottoms of your shoes?" I said, but I knew the answer and I gave it back to her: "You took that ring off Joan all right. You followed Joan out of the house when she ran and you waited for her and then you shot her. Then you had to bend down to get the ring back and you accidentally stepped in the blood. You didn't know it because your shoes didn't leave a footprint on the gravel. The police searched your apartment, but they didn't find the shoes because you had them on. You tried to plant the gun on me for your own reasons and the rest is history."

"Fuck you," Sam said. She bared her teeth like she would have enjoyed taking me apart with her incisors and her fingernails.

The quiet woman's eyes got big. "Oh my, my, my," she said again. She looked at Barb. "Well, I'm glad we didn't apologize," the quiet woman said.

"That does it for me." Loud Barb set her chin. "And I can tell you now I am not surprised. But then I could see how you all would be surprised. Just goes to show you. Of course, I know a little about human nature."

"It will be good to know that justice is done," Barb's girlfriend said solemnly. "I could tell Joan had a strong sense of justice."

Sam snorted. She crossed her legs at the knee and made a face at the bottoms of her shoes. "Justice?" She laughed and the sound was dull and hollow. "You have got to be kidding. You people are out of your minds. What would you know about what Joan wanted? You've canonized her as some kind of lesbian free-love saint."

Sam got up from the couch and said, "Sometimes it's a pure wonder what people will buy. I'll tell you about Joan. She blackmailed Anya. She blackmailed me and Jesus knows who all else over the years. She slept with anything that had tits and moved. She used her politics as an excuse. She was a user. I gave and gave and when there wasn't any more she was going to throw me away and get someone else. I could see it. She'd just plain used me up. That night when she came home with Naomi, you were right, Virginia, I was going to kill myself for the humiliation of it and then something happened. Joan had given me a gun to have for protection, off-season when she wasn't around."

I was starting to get it. "So, you killed her with her own gun, and afterwards you could keep it or plant it on me without worrying that the registration would lead the police to you."

Sam looked up at me and nodded. "But I didn't plan it at first. The plan came later. I was sitting right here on the couch with the gun in my lap getting up my nerve and then I saw my friend in a blue gown with the cats rolling around her ankles. She sat down right where Naomi is now. She had the cats in her lap and she told me what I ought to do. Then she walked straight through that wall right there by the table. When she'd gone it was almost morning. I heard Joan on the stairs and I knew it was a sign. I followed her out and waited by the construction site for her to come back from the beach." Sam looked at me steadily and with a lot of malice.

When Naomi got up from the reading chair she was white as a ghost and she looked like a breeze could have knocked her over. "God." Naomi shook her head. "I just don't believe this." She sat back down again like her legs had given out. Everybody else was looking at Sam and I could tell she liked it. She was taking her time with the story. "It was dark and Joan ran fast," Sam said. "I didn't have to wait very long. And I called for her to come over from the street. Her eyes were wide open when I shot her in the head. She knew why she was dying and I'm not sorry for it. Somebody should have done it a long time ago." Sam looked at the bottom of her sneakers again and ran her hand along the sole. She smiled at the quiet woman and said, "That's justice for you."

I looked at the floor and Naomi shrugged. "If the shoe fits." Naomi was a piece of work.

I was wondering how we were going to stop Sam from getting away when I saw Harmon standing in the foyer with a set of handcuffs open and waiting. It was the first time I'd ever been happy to see him.

XXXIV

"Did you ever think maybe she was trying to frame you, Naomi?" I asked.

She was having a cigarette on the porch and looking like she needed one. I, myself, could have used a drink, but that was going to have to wait.

I said, "Think about this. You were with Joan the night she died and Sam knew it. Maybe she was hoping it would come out later and she was just trying to keep us here until it did. She knew Helen followed you in from the bar. Maybe I just seemed convenient after I found the body and you told her the police suspected me already. Did you ever think about that?" I said.

Naomi didn't answer. For once in her life, it seemed like she was all out of words.

Harmon came out of the guest house and sat by me on the porch. He smoothed down his oily hair and thanked us for our help. "Sorry we had to give you ladies such a hard time," he said. "But murder is murder, you understand." He laughed at his pun and then he sighed. "I can't get over Sam. No offense but I'd rather it have been one of you girls."

"None taken," I said. It was only half a lie.

Naomi asked what was going to happen to Sam as if she didn't know and Harmon shrugged. "There'll be a trial. I heard her confession at the end and we've got the shoes and I imagine you'll have to come back to testify."

I nodded.

"Probably this place will go up for sale," Harmon said. "I wouldn't mind having some of this furniture and that round frame picture that was on the wall in the dead girl's room."

I asked him which dead girl he meant, and he told me the first one.

"I'd like to have that picture with the lady and those white cats," Harmon said and I asked him if he knew who she was.

He shook his head. "That lady was way before my time," Harmon said, "but I'd like the frame. I've got a picture of my wife when we were first married. I'd like to put my wife's picture in that old frame." He stood and hitched up his pants with his thumbs. "That old blue lady won't mind. She's probably already on her way to somewhere else."

A few of the publications of
THE NAIAD PRESS, INC.
P.O. Box 10543 • Tallahassee, Florida 32302
Phone (904) 539-5965
Toll-Free Order Number: 1-800-533-1973
Mail orders welcome. Please include 15% postage.

MICHAELA by Sarah Aldridge. 256 pp. A "Sarah Aldridge" romance. ISBN 1-56280-055-8 $10.95

KEEPING SECRETS by Penny Mickelbury. 208 pp. A Gianna Maglione Mystery. First in a series. ISBN 1-56280-052-3   9.95

THE ROMANTIC NAIAD edited by Katherine V. Forrest & Barbara Grier. 336 pp. Love stories by Naiad Press women. ISBN 1-56280-054-X   14.95

UNDER MY SKIN by Jaye Maiman. 336 pp. A Robin Miller mystery. 3rd in a series. ISBN 1-56280-049-3.   10.95

STAY TOONED by Rhonda Dicksion. 144 pp. Cartoons — 1st collection since *Lesbian Survival Manual.* ISBN 1-56280-045-0   9.95

CAR POOL by Karin Kallmaker. 272pp. Lesbians on wheels and then some! ISBN 1-56280-048-5   9.95

NOT TELLING MOTHER: STORIES FROM A LIFE by Diane Salvatore. 176 pp. Her 3rd novel. ISBN 1-56280-044-2   9.95

GOBLIN MARKET by Lauren Wright Douglas. 240pp. A Caitlin Reece Mystery. 5th in a series. ISBN 1-56280-047-7   9.95

LONG GOODBYES by Nikki Baker. 256 pp. A Virginia Kelly mystery. 3rd in a series. ISBN 1-56280-042-6   9.95

FRIENDS AND LOVERS by Jackie Calhoun. 224 pp. Mid-western Lesbian lives and loves. ISBN 1-56280-041-8   9.95

THE CAT CAME BACK by Hilary Mullins. 208 pp. Highly praised Lesbian novel. ISBN 1-56280-040-X   9.95

BEHIND CLOSED DOORS by Robbi Sommers. 192 pp. Hot, erotic short stories. ISBN 1-56280-039-6   9.95

CLAIRE OF THE MOON by Nicole Conn. 192 pp. See the movie — read the book! ISBN 1-56280-038-8   10.95

SILENT HEART by Claire McNab. 192 pp. Exotic Lesbian romance. ISBN 1-56280-036-1   9.95

HAPPY ENDINGS by Kate Brandt. 272 pp. Intimate conversations with Lesbian authors. ISBN 1-56280-050-7   10.95

THE SPY IN QUESTION by Amanda Kyle Williams. 256 pp. 4th
Madison McGuire.   ISBN 1-56280-037-X   9.95

SAVING GRACE by Jennifer Fulton. 240 pp. Adventure and
romantic entanglement.   ISBN 1-56280-051-5   9.95

THE YEAR SEVEN by Molleen Zanger. 208 pp. Women surviving
in a new world.   ISBN 1-56280-034-5   9.95

CURIOUS WINE by Katherine V. Forrest. 176 pp. Tenth
Anniversary Edition. The most popular contemporary Lesbian
love story.   ISBN 1-56280-053-1   9.95

CHAUTAUQUA by Catherine Ennis. 192 pp. Exciting, romantic
adventure.   ISBN 1-56280-032-9   9.95

A PROPER BURIAL by Pat Welch. 192 pp. A Helen Black
mystery. 3rd in a series.   ISBN 1-56280-033-7   9.95

SILVERLAKE HEAT: A Novel of Suspense by Carol Schmidt.
240 pp. Rhonda is as hot as Laney's dreams.   ISBN 1-56280-031-0   9.95

LOVE, ZENA BETH by Diane Salvatore. 224 pp. The most talked
about lesbian novel of the nineties!   ISBN 1-56280-030-2   9.95

A DOORYARD FULL OF FLOWERS by Isabel Miller. 160 pp.
Stories incl. 2 sequels to *Patience and Sarah.*   ISBN 1-56280-029-9   9.95

MURDER BY TRADITION by Katherine V. Forrest. 288 pp. A
Kate Delafield Mystery. 4th in a series.   ISBN 1-56280-002-7   9.95

THE EROTIC NAIAD edited by Katherine V. Forrest & Barbara Grier.
224 pp. Love stories by Naiad Press authors.   ISBN 1-56280-026-4   12.95

DEAD CERTAIN by Claire McNab. 224 pp. A Carol Ashton
mystery. 5th in a series.   ISBN 1-56280-027-2   9.95

CRAZY FOR LOVING by Jaye Maiman. 320 pp. A Robin Miller
mystery. 2nd in a series.   ISBN 1-56280-025-6   9.95

STONEHURST by Barbara Johnson. 176 pp. Passionate regency
romance.   ISBN 1-56280-024-8   9.95

INTRODUCING AMANDA VALENTINE by Rose Beecham.
256 pp. An Amanda Valentine Mystery. First in a series.
                                                ISBN 1-56280-021-3   9.95

UNCERTAIN COMPANIONS by Robbi Sommers. 204 pp.
Steamy, erotic novel.   ISBN 1-56280-017-5   9.95

A TIGER'S HEART by Lauren W. Douglas. 240 pp. A Caitlin
Reece mystery. 4th in a series.   ISBN 1-56280-018-3   9.95

PAPERBACK ROMANCE by Karin Kallmaker. 256 pp. A
delicious romance.   ISBN 1-56280-019-1   9.95

MORTON RIVER VALLEY by Lee Lynch. 304 pp. Lee Lynch at
her best!   ISBN 1-56280-016-7   9.95

THE LAVENDER HOUSE MURDER by Nikki Baker. 224 pp. A
Virginia Kelly Mystery. 2nd in a series.   ISBN 1-56280-012-4   9.95

PASSION BAY by Jennifer Fulton. 224 pp. Passionate romance,
virgin beaches, tropical skies.   ISBN 1-56280-028-0   9.95

STICKS AND STONES by Jackie Calhoun. 208 pp. Contemporary
lesbian lives and loves.   ISBN 1-56280-020-5   9.95

DELIA IRONFOOT by Jeane Harris. 192 pp. Adventure for Delia
and Beth in the Utah mountains.   ISBN 1-56280-014-0   9.95

UNDER THE SOUTHERN CROSS by Claire McNab. 192 pp.
Romantic nights Down Under.   ISBN 1-56280-011-6   9.95

RIVERFINGER WOMEN by Elana Nachman/Dykewomon.
208 pp. Classic Lesbian/feminist novel.   ISBN 1-56280-013-2   8.95

A CERTAIN DISCONTENT by Cleve Boutell. 240 pp. A unique
coterie of women.   ISBN 1-56280-009-4   9.95

GRASSY FLATS by Penny Hayes. 256 pp. Lesbian romance in
the '30s.   ISBN 1-56280-010-8   9.95

A SINGULAR SPY by Amanda K. Williams. 192 pp. 3rd Madison
McGuire.   ISBN 1-56280-008-6   8.95

THE END OF APRIL by Penny Sumner. 240 pp. A Victoria Cross
Mystery. First in a series.   ISBN 1-56280-007-8   8.95

A FLIGHT OF ANGELS by Sarah Aldridge. 240 pp. Romance set at
the National Gallery of Art   ISBN 1-56280-001-9   9.95

HOUSTON TOWN by Deborah Powell. 208 pp. A Hollis Carpenter
mystery. Second in a series.   ISBN 1-56280-006-X   8.95

KISS AND TELL by Robbi Sommers. 192 pp. Scorching stories by
the author of *Pleasures*.   ISBN 1-56280-005-1   9.95

STILL WATERS by Pat Welch. 208 pp. A Helen Black mystery.
2nd in a series.   ISBN 0-941483-97-5   9.95

TO LOVE AGAIN by Evelyn Kennedy. 208 pp. Wildly
romantic love story.   ISBN 0-941483-85-1   9.95

IN THE GAME by Nikki Baker. 192 pp. A Virginia Kelly
mystery. First in a series.   ISBN 01-56280-004-3   9.95

AVALON by Mary Jane Jones. 256 pp. A Lesbian Arthurian
romance.   ISBN 0-941483-96-7   9.95

STRANDED by Camarin Grae. 320 pp. Entertaining, riveting
adventure.   ISBN 0-941483-99-1   9.95

THE DAUGHTERS OF ARTEMIS by Lauren Wright Douglas.
240 pp. A Caitlin Reece mystery. 3rd in a series.
                                  ISBN 0-941483-95-9   9.95

CLEARWATER by Catherine Ennis. 176 pp. Romantic secrets
of a small Louisiana town.   ISBN 0-941483-65-7   8.95

THE HALLELUJAH MURDERS by Dorothy Tell. 176 pp. A Poppy
Dillworth mystery. 2nd in a series.   ISBN 0-941483-88-6   8.95

ZETA BASE by Judith Alguire. 208 pp. Lesbian triangle
on a future Earth.   ISBN 0-941483-94-0   9.95

SECOND CHANCE by Jackie Calhoun. 256 pp. Contemporary
Lesbian lives and loves.   ISBN 0-941483-93-2   9.95

BENEDICTION by Diane Salvatore. 272 pp. Striking,
contemporary romantic novel.   ISBN 0-941483-90-8   9.95

CALLING RAIN by Karen Marie Christa Minns. 240 pp.
Spellbinding, erotic love story   ISBN 0-941483-87-8   9.95

BLACK IRIS by Jeane Harris. 192 pp. Caroline's hidden past . . .
                                      ISBN 0-941483-68-1   8.95

TOUCHWOOD by Karin Kallmaker. 240 pp. Loving, May/
December romance.   ISBN 0-941483-76-2   9.95

BAYOU CITY SECRETS by Deborah Powell. 224 pp. A Hollis
Carpenter mystery. First in a series. ISBN 0-941483-91-6   9.95

COP OUT by Claire McNab. 208 pp. A Carol Ashton mystery.
4th in a series.   ISBN 0-941483-84-3   9.95

LODESTAR by Phyllis Horn. 224 pp. Romantic, fast-moving
adventure.   ISBN 0-941483-83-5   8.95

THE BEVERLY MALIBU by Katherine V. Forrest. 288 pp. A
Kate Delafield Mystery. 3rd in a series.   ISBN 0-941483-48-7   9.95

THAT OLD STUDEBAKER by Lee Lynch. 272 pp. Andy's affair
with Regina and her attachment to her beloved car.
                                      ISBN 0-941483-82-7   9.95

PASSION'S LEGACY by Lori Paige. 224 pp. Sarah is swept into
the arms of Augusta Pym in this delightful historical romance.
                                      ISBN 0-941483-81-9   8.95

THE PROVIDENCE FILE by Amanda Kyle Williams. 256 pp.
Second Madison McGuire   ISBN 0-941483-92-4   8.95

I LEFT MY HEART by Jaye Maiman. 320 pp. A Robin Miller
Mystery. First in a series.   ISBN 0-941483-72-X   9.95

THE PRICE OF SALT by Patricia Highsmith (writing as Claire
Morgan). 288 pp. Classic lesbian novel, first issued in 1952 . . .
acknowledged by its author under her own, very famous, name.
                                      ISBN 1-56280-003-5   9.95

SIDE BY SIDE by Isabel Miller. 256 pp. From beloved author of
Patience and Sarah.   ISBN 0-941483-77-0   9.95

STAYING POWER: LONG TERM LESBIAN COUPLES
by Susan E. Johnson. 352 pp. Joys of coupledom.
                                      ISBN 0-941-483-75-4   12.95

SLICK by Camarin Grae. 304 pp. Exotic, erotic adventure.
                                      ISBN 0-941483-74-6   9.95

NINTH LIFE by Lauren Wright Douglas. 256 pp. A Caitlin
Reece mystery. 2nd in a series.   ISBN 0-941483-50-9   8.95

PLAYERS by Robbi Sommers. 192 pp. Sizzling, erotic novel.
ISBN 0-941483-73-8   9.95

MURDER AT RED ROOK RANCH by Dorothy Tell. 224 pp.
A Poppy Dillworth mystery. 1st in a series.   ISBN 0-941483-80-0   8.95

LESBIAN SURVIVAL MANUAL by Rhonda Dicksion.
112 pp. Cartoons!   ISBN 0-941483-71-1   8.95

A ROOM FULL OF WOMEN by Elisabeth Nonas. 256 pp.
Contemporary Lesbian lives.   ISBN 0-941483-69-X   9.95

PRIORITIES by Lynda Lyons 288 pp. Science fiction with
a twist.   ISBN 0-941483-66-5   8.95

THEME FOR DIVERSE INSTRUMENTS by Jane Rule. 208
pp. Powerful romantic lesbian stories.   ISBN 0-941483-63-0   8.95

LESBIAN QUERIES by Hertz & Ertman. 112 pp. The questions
you were too embarrassed to ask.   ISBN 0-941483-67-3   8.95

CLUB 12 by Amanda Kyle Williams. 288 pp. Espionage thriller
featuring a lesbian agent!   ISBN 0-941483-64-9   8.95

DEATH DOWN UNDER by Claire McNab. 240 pp. A Carol
Ashton mystery. 3rd in a series.   ISBN 0-941483-39-8   9.95

MONTANA FEATHERS by Penny Hayes. 256 pp. Vivian and
Elizabeth find love in frontier Montana.   ISBN 0-941483-61-4   8.95

CHESAPEAKE PROJECT by Phyllis Horn. 304 pp. Jessie &
Meredith in perilous adventure.   ISBN 0-941483-58-4   8.95

LIFESTYLES by Jackie Calhoun. 224 pp. Contemporary Lesbian
lives and loves.   ISBN 0-941483-57-6   9.95

VIRAGO by Karen Marie Christa Minns. 208 pp. Darsen has
chosen Ginny.   ISBN 0-941483-56-8   8.95

WILDERNESS TREK by Dorothy Tell. 192 pp. Six women on
vacation learning ''new'' skills.   ISBN 0-941483-60-6   8.95

MURDER BY THE BOOK by Pat Welch. 256 pp. A Helen
Black Mystery. First in a series.   ISBN 0-941483-59-2   9.95

LESBIANS IN GERMANY by Lillian Faderman & B. Eriksson.
128 pp. Fiction, poetry, essays.   ISBN 0-941483-62-2   8.95

THERE'S SOMETHING I'VE BEEN MEANING TO TELL
YOU Ed. by Loralee MacPike. 288 pp. Gay men and lesbians
coming out to their children.   ISBN 0-941483-44-4   9.95

LIFTING BELLY by Gertrude Stein. Ed. by Rebecca Mark. 104
pp. Erotic poetry.   ISBN 0-941483-51-7   8.95

ROSE PENSKI by Roz Perry. 192 pp. Adult lovers in a long-term
relationship.   ISBN 0-941483-37-1   8.95

AFTER THE FIRE by Jane Rule. 256 pp. Warm, human novel
by this incomparable author.   ISBN 0-941483-45-2   8.95

SUE SLATE, PRIVATE EYE by Lee Lynch. 176 pp. The gay
folk of Peacock Alley are *all cats.*   ISBN 0-941483-52-5   8.95

CHRIS by Randy Salem. 224 pp. Golden oldie. Handsome Chris
and her adventures.   ISBN 0-941483-42-8   8.95

THREE WOMEN by March Hastings. 232 pp. Golden oldie. A
triangle among wealthy sophisticates.   ISBN 0-941483-43-6   8.95

RICE AND BEANS by Valeria Taylor. 232 pp. Love and
romance on poverty row.   ISBN 0-941483-41-X   8.95

PLEASURES by Robbi Sommers. 204 pp. Unprecedented
eroticism.   ISBN 0-941483-49-5   8.95

EDGEWISE by Camarin Grae. 372 pp. Spellbinding
adventure.   ISBN 0-941483-19-3   9.95

FATAL REUNION by Claire McNab. 224 pp. A Carol Ashton
mystery. 2nd in a series.   ISBN 0-941483-40-1   8.95

KEEP TO ME STRANGER by Sarah Aldridge. 372 pp. Romance
set in a department store dynasty.   ISBN 0-941483-38-X   9.95

HEARTSCAPE by Sue Gambill. 204 pp. American lesbian in
Portugal.   ISBN 0-941483-33-9   8.95

IN THE BLOOD by Lauren Wright Douglas. 252 pp. Lesbian
science fiction adventure fantasy   ISBN 0-941483-22-3   8.95

THE BEE'S KISS by Shirley Verel. 216 pp. Delicate, delicious
romance.   ISBN 0-941483-36-3   8.95

RAGING MOTHER MOUNTAIN by Pat Emmerson. 264 pp.
Furosa Firechild's adventures in Wonderland.   ISBN 0-941483-35-5   8.95

IN EVERY PORT by Karin Kallmaker. 228 pp. Jessica's sexy,
adventuresome travels.   ISBN 0-941483-37-7   9.95

OF LOVE AND GLORY by Evelyn Kennedy. 192 pp. Exciting
WWII romance.   ISBN 0-941483-32-0   8.95

CLICKING STONES by Nancy Tyler Glenn. 288 pp. Love
transcending time.   ISBN 0-941483-31-2   9.95

SURVIVING SISTERS by Gail Pass. 252 pp. Powerful love
story.   ISBN 0-941483-16-9   8.95

SOUTH OF THE LINE by Catherine Ennis. 216 pp. Civil War
adventure.   ISBN 0-941483-29-0   8.95

WOMAN PLUS WOMAN by Dolores Klaich. 300 pp. Supurb
Lesbian overview.   ISBN 0-941483-28-2   9.95

HEAVY GILT by Delores Klaich. 192 pp. Lesbian detective/
disappearing homophobes/upper class gay society.

                                                  ISBN 0-941483-25-8   8.95

THE FINER GRAIN by Denise Ohio. 216 pp. Brilliant young
college lesbian novel.   ISBN 0-941483-11-8   8.95

THE AMAZON TRAIL by Lee Lynch. 216 pp. Life, travel & lore
of famous lesbian author.   ISBN 0-941483-27-4   8.95

HIGH CONTRAST by Jessie Lattimore. 264 pp. Women of the
Crystal Palace.   ISBN 0-941483-17-7   8.95

OCTOBER OBSESSION by Meredith More. Josie's rich, secret
Lesbian life.   ISBN 0-941483-18-5   8.95

LESBIAN CROSSROADS by Ruth Baetz. 276 pp. Contemporary
Lesbian lives.   ISBN 0-941483-21-5   9.95

BEFORE STONEWALL: THE MAKING OF A GAY AND
LESBIAN COMMUNITY by Andrea Weiss & Greta Schiller.
96 pp., 25 illus.   ISBN 0-941483-20-7   7.95

WE WALK THE BACK OF THE TIGER by Patricia A. Murphy.
192 pp. Romantic Lesbian novel/beginning women's movement.
                                             ISBN 0-941483-13-4   8.95

SUNDAY'S CHILD by Joyce Bright. 216 pp. Lesbian athletics, at
last the novel about sports.   ISBN 0-941483-12-6   8.95

OSTEN'S BAY by Zenobia N. Vole. 204 pp. Sizzling adventure
romance set on Bonaire.   ISBN 0-941483-15-0   8.95

LESSONS IN MURDER by Claire McNab. 216 pp. A Carol
Ashton mystery. First in a series.   ISBN 0-941483-14-2   9.95

YELLOWTHROAT by Penny Hayes. 240 pp. Margarita, bandit,
kidnaps Julia.   ISBN 0-941483-10-X   8.95

SAPPHISTRY: THE BOOK OF LESBIAN SEXUALITY by
Pat Califia. 3d edition, revised. 208 pp.   ISBN 0-941483-24-X   10.95

CHERISHED LOVE by Evelyn Kennedy. 192 pp. Erotic
Lesbian love story.   ISBN 0-941483-08-8   9.95

LAST SEPTEMBER by Helen R. Hull. 208 pp. Six stories & a
glorious novella.   ISBN 0-941483-09-6   8.95

THE SECRET IN THE BIRD by Camarin Grae. 312 pp. Striking,
psychological suspense novel.   ISBN 0-941483-05-3   8.95

TO THE LIGHTNING by Catherine Ennis. 208 pp. Romantic
Lesbian 'Robinson Crusoe' adventure.   ISBN 0-941483-06-1   8.95

THE OTHER SIDE OF VENUS by Shirley Verel. 224 pp.
Luminous, romantic love story.   ISBN 0-941483-07-X   8.95

DREAMS AND SWORDS by Katherine V. Forrest. 192 pp.
Romantic, erotic, imaginative stories.   ISBN 0-941483-03-7   8.95

MEMORY BOARD by Jane Rule. 336 pp. Memorable novel
about an aging Lesbian couple.   ISBN 0-941483-02-9   9.95

THE ALWAYS ANONYMOUS BEAST by Lauren Wright
Douglas. 224 pp. A Caitlin Reece mystery. First in a series.
                                             ISBN 0-941483-04-5   8.95

SEARCHING FOR SPRING by Patricia A. Murphy. 224 pp.
Novel about the recovery of love.   ISBN 0-941483-00-2   **8.95**

DUSTY'S QUEEN OF HEARTS DINER by Lee Lynch. 240 pp.
Romantic blue-collar novel.   ISBN 0-941483-01-0   **8.95**

PARENTS MATTER by Ann Muller. 240 pp. Parents'
relationships with Lesbian daughters and gay sons.
     ISBN 0-930044-91-6   **9.95**

THE PEARLS by Shelley Smith. 176 pp. Passion and fun in
the Caribbean sun.   ISBN 0-930044-93-2   **7.95**

MAGDALENA by Sarah Aldridge. 352 pp. Epic Lesbian novel
set on three continents.   ISBN 0-930044-99-1   **8.95**

THE BLACK AND WHITE OF IT by Ann Allen Shockley.
144 pp. Short stories.   ISBN 0-930044-96-7   **7.95**

SAY JESUS AND COME TO ME by Ann Allen Shockley. 288
pp. Contemporary romance.   ISBN 0-930044-98-3   **8.95**

LOVING HER by Ann Allen Shockley. 192 pp. Romantic love
story.   ISBN 0-930044-97-5   **7.95**

MURDER AT THE NIGHTWOOD BAR by Katherine V.
Forrest. 240 pp. A Kate Delafield mystery. Second in a series.
     ISBN 0-930044-92-4   **9.95**

ZOE'S BOOK by Gail Pass. 224 pp. Passionate, obsessive love
story.   ISBN 0-930044-95-9   **7.95**

WINGED DANCER by Camarin Grae. 228 pp. Erotic Lesbian
adventure story.   ISBN 0-930044-88-6   **8.95**

PAZ by Camarin Grae. 336 pp. Romantic Lesbian adventurer
with the power to change the world.   ISBN 0-930044-89-4   **8.95**

SOUL SNATCHER by Camarin Grae. 224 pp. A puzzle, an
adventure, a mystery — Lesbian romance.   ISBN 0-930044-90-8   **8.95**

THE LOVE OF GOOD WOMEN by Isabel Miller. 224 pp.
Long-awaited new novel by the author of the beloved *Patience
and Sarah.*   ISBN 0-930044-81-9   **8.95**

THE HOUSE AT PELHAM FALLS by Brenda Weathers. 240
pp. Suspenseful Lesbian ghost story.   ISBN 0-930044-79-7   **7.95**

HOME IN YOUR HANDS by Lee Lynch. 240 pp. More stories
from the author of *Old Dyke Tales.*   ISBN 0-930044-80-0   **7.95**

SURPLUS by Sylvia Stevenson. 342 pp. A classic early Lesbian
novel.   ISBN 0-930044-78-9   **7.95**

PEMBROKE PARK by Michelle Martin. 256 pp. Derring-do
and daring romance in Regency England.   ISBN 0-930044-77-0   **7.95**

THE LONG TRAIL by Penny Hayes. 248 pp. Vivid adventures
of two women in love in the old west.   ISBN 0-930044-76-2   **8.95**

AN EMERGENCE OF GREEN by Katherine V. Forrest. 288
pp. Powerful novel of sexual discovery.   ISBN 0-930044-69-X   9.95

THE LESBIAN PERIODICALS INDEX edited by Claire
Potter. 432 pp. Author & subject index.   ISBN 0-930044-74-6   12.95

DESERT OF THE HEART by Jane Rule. 224 pp. A classic;
basis for the movie *Desert Hearts*.   ISBN 0-930044-73-8   9.95

FOR KEEPS by Elisabeth Nonas. 144 pp. Contemporary novel
about losing and finding love.   ISBN 0-930044-71-1   7.95

TORCHLIGHT TO VALHALLA by Gale Wilhelm. 128 pp.
Classic novel by a great Lesbian writer.   ISBN 0-930044-68-1   7.95

LESBIAN NUNS: BREAKING SILENCE edited by Rosemary
Curb and Nancy Manahan. 432 pp. Unprecedented autobiographies
of religious life.   ISBN 0-930044-62-2   9.95

THE SWASHBUCKLER by Lee Lynch. 288 pp. Colorful novel
set in Greenwich Village in the sixties.   ISBN 0-930044-66-5   8.95

MISFORTUNE'S FRIEND by Sarah Aldridge. 320 pp. Historical Lesbian novel set on two continents.   ISBN 0-930044-67-3   7.95

SEX VARIANT WOMEN IN LITERATURE by Jeannette
Howard Foster. 448 pp. Literary history.   ISBN 0-930044-65-7   8.95

A HOT-EYED MODERATE by Jane Rule. 252 pp. Hard-hitting
essays on gay life; writing; art.   ISBN 0-930044-57-6   7.95

WE TOO ARE DRIFTING by Gale Wilhelm. 128 pp. Timeless
Lesbian novel, a masterpiece.   ISBN 0-930044-61-4   6.95

AMATEUR CITY by Katherine V. Forrest. 224 pp. A Kate
Delafield mystery. First in a series.   ISBN 0-930044-55-X   9.95

THE SOPHIE HOROWITZ STORY by Sarah Schulman. 176
pp. Engaging novel of madcap intrigue.   ISBN 0-930044-54-1   7.95

THE YOUNG IN ONE ANOTHER'S ARMS by Jane Rule.
224 pp. Classic Jane Rule.   ISBN 0-930044-53-3   9.95

OLD DYKE TALES by Lee Lynch. 224 pp. Extraordinary
stories of our diverse Lesbian lives.   ISBN 0-930044-51-7   8.95

DAUGHTERS OF A CORAL DAWN by Katherine V. Forrest.
240 pp. Novel set in a Lesbian new world.   ISBN 0-930044-50-9   9.95

AGAINST THE SEASON by Jane Rule. 224 pp. Luminous,
complex novel of interrelationships.   ISBN 0-930044-48-7   8.95

LOVERS IN THE PRESENT AFTERNOON by Kathleen
Fleming. 288 pp. A novel about recovery and growth.
   ISBN 0-930044-46-0   8.95

TOOTHPICK HOUSE by Lee Lynch. 264 pp. Love between
two Lesbians of different classes.   ISBN 0-930044-45-2   7.95

MADAME AURORA by Sarah Aldridge. 256 pp. Historical
novel featuring a charismatic "seer."   ISBN 0-930044-44-4   7.95

CONTRACT WITH THE WORLD by Jane Rule. 340 pp.
Powerful, panoramic novel of gay life.   ISBN 0-930044-28-2   9.95

THE NESTING PLACE by Sarah Aldridge. 224 pp. A
three-woman triangle — love conquers all!   ISBN 0-930044-26-6   7.95

THIS IS NOT FOR YOU by Jane Rule. 284 pp. A letter to a
beloved is also an intricate novel.   ISBN 0-930044-25-8   8.95

ANNA'S COUNTRY by Elizabeth Lang. 208 pp. A woman
finds her Lesbian identity.   ISBN 0-930044-19-3   8.95

PRISM by Valerie Taylor. 158 pp. A love affair between two
women in their sixties.   ISBN 0-930044-18-5   6.95

OUTLANDER by Jane Rule. 207 pp. Short stories and essays
by one of our finest writers.   ISBN 0-930044-17-7   8.95

ALL TRUE LOVERS by Sarah Aldridge. 292 pp. Romantic
novel set in the 1930s and 1940s.   ISBN 0-930044-10-X   8.95

CYTHEREA'S BREATH by Sarah Aldridge. 240 pp. Romantic
novel about women's entrance into medicine.
                                                 ISBN 0-930044-02-9   6.95

TOTTIE by Sarah Aldridge. 181 pp. Lesbian romance in the
turmoil of the sixties.   ISBN 0-930044-01-0   6.95

THE LATECOMER by Sarah Aldridge. 107 pp. A delicate love
story.   ISBN 0-930044-00-2   6.95

ODD GIRL OUT by Ann Bannon.   ISBN 0-930044-83-5   5.95
I AM A WOMAN 84-3; WOMEN IN THE SHADOWS 85-1;   each
JOURNEY TO A WOMAN 86-X; BEEBO BRINKER 87-8. Golden
oldies about life in Greenwich Village.

JOURNEY TO FULFILLMENT, A WORLD WITHOUT MEN, and   3.95
RETURN TO LESBOS. All by Valerie Taylor   each

These are just a few of the many Naiad Press titles — we are the oldest and
largest lesbian/feminist publishing company in the world. Please request a
complete catalog. We offer personal service; we encourage and welcome direct
mail orders from individuals who have limited access to bookstores carrying
our publications.